TOTO
THE NINJA CAT
AND THE MYSTERY
JEWEL THIEF

DERMOT O'LEARY

ILLUSTRATED BY NICK EAST

HODDER

HODDER CHILDREN'S BOOKS

First published in Great Britain in 2020 by Hodder & Stoughton Limited
This paperback edition published in 2021 by Hodder & Stoughton Limited

5 7 9 10 8 6

Text copyright © Dermot O'Leary, 2020
Illustrations copyright © Nick East, 2020
Inside back cover photograph by Ray Burmiston

A CIP catalogue record for this book
is available from the British Library.

ISBN 978 1 444 95208 7

Printed and bound in Great Britain by Clays Ltd, Elcograf S.p.A.
The paper and board used in this book are made from wood from
responsible sources

Hodder Children's Books
An imprint of Hachette Children's Group
Part of Hodder & Stoughton Limited
Carmelite House
50 Victoria Embankment
London EC4Y 0DZ
An Hachette UK Company
www.hachette.co.uk
www.hachettechildrens.co.uk

TO PIP
I PROMISE TO DO MY BEST, TO FILL YOUR
WORLD WITH STORIES AND WONDER ...
SO LONG AS YOU SLEEP THROUGH THE NIGHT

PROLOGUE

It was gone midnight when Mayor Dick Whittington, riding a giant horse and with his trusty cat companion, Tom, tucked inside his coat, finally arrived at his destination: the top of **HAMPSTEAD HEATH,** the highest point in the

1

whole of **MEDIEVAL LONDON**.

Overlooking the capital, they could easily make out St Paul's Cathedral, standing proudly, the beacon for all Londoners, its tall spire jutting up into the cold clear night sky.

For a while, they said nothing, content to take in the view of the city they had helped to build and keep safe.

With a quiet purr, Tom finally emerged from his master's coat, climbed out and stretched, arching his back. He then nuzzled at Dick's neck, before jumping down effortlessly from the horse on to the mossy grass below.

Both Dick and Tom were exhausted, but this task had to be **COMPLETED IN SECRET,** under the cover of darkness. This was partly due to their fame (in late medieval London, everyone knew the Mayor and his cat) but also due to the importance and power of what Tom carried with him.

'Are you sure about this, Tom?' Dick whispered as loudly as he dared, afraid of being overheard. 'You won it fair and square by **DEFEATING AN EVIL** that would have plagued this city, maybe even the whole country. **KING RODERICK THE ABSOLUTELY FILTHY DIRTY** is beaten and his rat army have fled thanks to you. Now with this **MYSTERIOUS, MAGICAL COLLAR** you're the most **POWERFUL ANIMAL IN THE WORLD!** Because of the strength it gives you, no one can best you in combat and, most incredibly, you can speak to me in my tongue.'

'Don't you think I know that, my old friend?' the wise cat replied. 'That's all the more reason to do what I do tonight. I can't risk this collar falling into dangerous hands. The animal world is safe for now, but should this collar be found by the wrong cat, rat or dog ... Now, come and join me – it's time.'

His master dismounted and dug out a small silver box from his horse's saddle bag. He carried it over to Tom, and they stood together at the side of a pond.

The human smiled at his companion. 'I'll miss our chats, Tom.'

'Oh, don't worry, Dick, I'll still understand you, but now I won't have to answer back. I can act like a regular cat and ignore you!'

Dick laughed and ruffled Tom's fur. 'Well, if you are sure this is the right thing to do, rest assured, I'll honour our agreement: half will go to the Tower of London, and half will be lost for all time.'

The cat nodded and pawed at the collar. It unclasped and came apart into two perfect circles – one of flawless diamonds and one of deep blue sapphires – shining in the moonlight. No matter how many times they saw it, both human and cat found its beauty staggering.

Taking one last look, **TOM PLACED THE DIAMOND BAND** into a velvet pouch and carefully popped it back into the **SILVER BOX**. Snapping it shut, he threw it into the deep inky pond, and they watched it slowly sink to the bottom, eventually disappearing from sight.

THE TWO FRIENDS SMILED AT EACH OTHER. Although Tom felt sad that he'd never get to speak in the human tongue again, it was a small price to pay.

He jumped up into the warmth of his master's coat, and they mounted the horse and started the ride back into London and their cosy beds. Tom was certain that, with his enemies beaten, all the animals of old London town, and indeed **THE WORLD, WOULD BE SAFE** ... and so they were for the next 600 years.

UNTIL ...

CHAPTER 1

'RATTY DAYS ARE HEEERRREEE AGAIIINNNNNNNN, yes they are, yes they are, oooohhhh bbbabyyy!' the singer blasted out, as he finished his set with a bow.

'You've been a great audience, thank you and good night!' he called to the wild crowd.

'*CATFACE, CATFACE, CATFACE!*' they chanted, as he wiped the sweat from his brow, waved to the adoring throng one last time and made his way off stage.

TOTO THE NINJA CAT and the gang had come to see their friend play at the legendary *PAWS ROBINSON JAZZ AND MILK BAR IN SOHO IN LONDON*. All the hippest cats, dogs, ferrets, foxes and even pigeons were here tonight. Paws Robinson welcomed every kind of animal – you just had to be cool, which meant: be true to your animal self; no cat or any other kind of fights; love your neighbour; and love your music. This was certainly the place to be.

Toto was enjoying the last night off she'd be having for a while. Tomorrow some human diplomats would be arriving from France, and their animal equivalents would be coming with them. So, she'd be on duty looking after the **FRENCH ANIMAL AMBASSADOR** Monsieur Raton Laveur.

For Toto and her boss, Larry, babysitting animal diplomats would be an easy security assignment, and after all the adventures she'd had since becoming a fully fledged **NINJA CAT,** 'easy' sounded just fine.

Catface had made his way down the stairs at the side of the stage, and was weaving his way across the floor to where his friends were seated at a candle-lit table. Dressed in a black roll-neck sweater and a midnight-blue velvet jacket, topped off with a beret and dark shades, he certainly looked the part of a jazz crooner!

Around the table with Toto were:

🐾 Her cheeky, but brave and **loyal brother Silver**, who, because Toto was almost totally blind, acted as her eyes and considered himself to be her deputy – even though he unintentionally caused as many problems as he solved!

🐾 Her newly **adopted brother Socks**, who'd joined the family from Battersea Dogs & Cats Home, although he still kept in touch

with his gang of street urchins:
the Battersea Bruisers

🐾 **Toto's boss Larry**, head of the
UK branch of the Ancient Order
of International Ninja Cats

🐾 And their police dog friend, **Sheila
Snarlingfoot**, who was head of
Criminal Investigation Animals
(CIA) and had been put in charge
of planning security during the
ambassador's visit

As Catface slid into a chair, a huge, fluffy,
brown-and-red cat wearing a fedora hat
appeared behind him.

'Catface, my friend, *THAT WAS IMMENSE* ... wild set,' he drawled in an American accent.

Everyone gasped as they realised it was the legendary *PAWS ROBINSON HIMSELF!* He was the owner of the club and was one of the finest cat jazz musicians in the world.

'Y'all must come round again some time so I can have dinner with this crazy gang of misfits,' he said, and then put a huge, warm paw on Toto's shoulder.

'I heard about what you did to save Catstonbury Festival – we musicians owe you all our deepest gratitude. You keep up the good work with this fine gentleman.' He nodded to Larry, before calling out to a passing waiter: 'Drinks on the house for this here table. Now, if you'll excuse me, I gotta go play a set myself – been a pleasure speaking with y'all.'

'THE PAWS ROBINSON!' Silver blurted out as soon as Paws had mooched off towards the stage. 'Came to see us! Catface, you've arrived!'

'Oh, it's nothing really,' replied the rat. But he looked very pleased with himself as he leaned back in his chair and took a sip of his cold Jersey milk. 'You know my talent is as much a curse as anything else, but I'd hate to let my public down by hiding it away.'

'*CATFACE, THIS IS ONLY YOUR SIXTH GIG!*' Larry laughed, rolling his eyes.

That much was true, but since Catface had stepped in at the last minute to perform and help save the day at **CATSTONBURY,** his singing career had blossomed. Together with his band, **THE LONGTAILS,** he'd just been on a European tour playing in Rome, Berlin, Madrid and Paris. Tonight had been his homecoming gig in London.

While Catface had been away, Toto and Larry had remained on **HIGH ALERT**. Because even though Toto had once again defeated **ARCHDUKE FERDICAT** (before he could take over the animal world using a hypnotising music video), ADF had escaped and Toto had no idea where he had gone. There was no telling when or how he'd resurface. The streets had been pretty quiet, but they knew ADF would be busy plotting some new, even more evil plans. With his own unique style and charm!

'Well, I've had the most wonderful time being a musician, but I must say I'm looking forward to a day off tomorrow. I might do a spot of fishing – anyone care to join? Oh blast, you're all working, aren't you?' Catface asked his friends.

'I'm afraid so,' said Sheila. 'This lot are helping me with **SECURITY FOR THE FRENCH AMBASSADOR'S TRIP.** Thanks, by the way – I know it's not as glamorous as the adventures you Ninja Cats are used to.'

'More than happy to help out,' replied Larry cheerfully. 'We haven't seen hide nor hair of ADF since Catstonbury, and thanks to this one and her able deputies,' he said, nudging Toto, 'the streets are safer than they've ever been.'

This made Toto very happy; Larry was her mentor, her boss and her friend, so if he thought she was doing a good job, together with her brothers, then she couldn't be prouder.

'So, remind me what's on the itinerary?' she asked Sheila, leaning forward attentively in her chair.

'The usual really, as it'll shadow the human tour. There'll be a state banquet in the evening, a visit to the House of Commons and a twenty-one-meow salute. Oh, and there was one thing they were quite insistent on which I haven't been able to arrange so I really need your help: the ambassador would love to see the **CROWN JEWELS AT THE TOWER OF LONDON**, especially Old Tom's Collar. I told him we might not be able to accommodate him since the collar is so sacred but then I remembered you have one of the only two keys in the world that open the case, Larry – is that right?'

'Correct,' replied Larry. 'The other is held by the **CHIEF YEOMAN RAVEN CYRIL CORVUSTON.** He's been in the job for years and is as trustworthy as they come. Don't worry, he and I are old pals. I'm sure it won't be a problem.'

'Thanks so much.' Sheila sighed with relief. 'My boss has been on top of me about this, he's like a ... *cat* with a bone?'

'But I thought *you* were the boss?' asked a confused Toto.

'Well, sure. I run the animal police force, or CIA, which includes your average police dogs, an elite undercover unit of foxes, although they are useless around chickens, a flock of wood pigeons, mostly for transport, and a group of frogs led by my friend Anushka … they do the aquatic stuff. Like you Ninja Cats, we work with and for both animals and humans, though the humans obviously don't have a clue! But everyone's got a boss somewhere, right?'

'You've got that right,' piped up Silver. 'Ours is such a taskmaster, on our backs night and day – am I right, sis?' he said, nudging Toto while Larry gave a chuckle.

'Very funny, bro, I get it,' Toto answered, shaking her head at the terrible joke. 'Sorry, go on, Sheila – who's your boss?'

'Well, just as humans have their parliament that runs things, we have an animal parliament and my boss is our home secretary, *SIR WIGBERT FLUFFYPAWS THE THIRD—*'

At this, Larry interrupted to add, 'Toto, you should know that he's not a massive fan of us Ninja Cats. Always been jealous of my office at Downing Street, and he spouts a lot of nonsense about how we shouldn't be allowed to operate above the law. To be honest, he's a bit of an old fuddy-duddy. But it's important to take the higher ground, so don't be offended if he speaks down to us tomorrow.'

Toto nodded solemnly as Silver asked, '*WHAT EXACTLY IS SO SPECIAL ABOUT OLD TOM'S COLLAR?*'

Socks was the one to answer – having lived his whole life in London, he knew a lot more about the city than his adopted brother and sister, who had been born in Italy. 'Come on, bro, you must have heard the tale of Dick Whittington and his cat Tom? Came to London to find their fortune and Tom—'

'Helped Dick Whittington defeat an army of evil rats ... *Everyone* knows that – we're Italian, not stupid!' said Silver with a laugh.

'Yes, err, but times *HAVE* changed!' interjected Catface, a little hot under the collar. '*CATS, RATS, WE'RE ALL FRIENDS NOW!*'

'Well,' Socks continued, 'Old *TOM'S COLLAR* belonged to *that* Tom. It's proper valuable, the most precious of our animal crown jewels. The sapphires have got more sparkle than the glint in old Catface's eye!

It's been in the Tower as long as anyone can remember, guarded by them ravens. Nothing gets past them – smart as cats, razor-sharp beaks and talons like swords, expert flyers, as good as any swift or falcon. They are the elitist of elite. Present company excepted, guv.' He winked at Larry.

'Quite right, young Socks,' said Larry. 'And on that note, let's all get a good night's sleep. It should be pretty straightforward tomorrow, but we still need to be vigilant. Cats, I'll see you tomorrow; Catface, go easy on the milk and have a good day off.'

The team left the jazz club and went their separate ways, all feeling happy and confident that the following day would go smoothly. In truth, it would go anything but.

CHAPTER 2

So far, the tour had been nothing short of a stunning **SUCCESS IN DIPLOMACY,** and Sheila was over the moon. The sun had been shining, showing London off in all its glory. The twenty-one-meow salute had gone purrfectly, although the noise had terrified a nearby human milkman and made him crash his milk float.

Lunch had taken place below a cheese shop in Mayfair, and was a magnificent affair, with mountains of Brie, Camembert and gooey *tartiflette* (a French dish of cheese, potatoes, bacon and cream, which Silver *loved* – 'Unbelievable. I can die a happy cat, and I want to come back French! '). Although Sheila's boss, the stuffy old fusspot Sir Wigbert Fluffypaws the Third, had fallen asleep in his saucer of milk.

Early afternoon involved a quick visit to the animal parliament, which was just beneath the human House of Commons. There, they had watched a raging debate about pigeon poo ... apparently it was everywhere! **THE PIGEON EQUALITY PARTY** was up in arms, claiming it wasn't pigeons' fault because not every animal has a litter tray or owners with bags.

Now, all that was left before the state banquet was the visit to the **TOWER OF LONDON.** Toto was as excited as everyone else. Every kitten in the world knew the tale of **TOM AND DICK WHITTINGTON,** and even with her poor eyesight, she felt sure she'd be able to see some sparkling light reflecting off the sapphires. Though she couldn't help wondering why Larry hadn't mentioned that he looked after one of the keys before. *Top secret, I suppose*, she thought to herself.

Toto also couldn't help but think that one day *she* might be the holder of that key when Larry retired. And maybe, just maybe, she could try the collar on? OK, it wasn't strictly in the Ninja code, but there was no harm in being stylish!

The French ambassador, Monsieur Raton Laveur, was *very* stylish. He was a charming white rat, dressed impeccably in a cream pin-striped suit. Silver told Toto that Monsieur had much better dress sense than the Home Secretary, sleepy Sir Fluffypaws the Third, who was an old ginger cat with a massive moustache. He was dressed in an old-fashioned three-piece woollen suit and sported a monocle.

In addition to these two, the party was made up of:

🐾 A dozen or so of **Monsieur Laveur's staff**, who were a mixture of equally well-turned-out cats and rats

🐾 **Sheila** and her **squad of beefy-looking Alsatian police dogs**

🐾 **Larry and Toto**, of course, plus **Silver** and **Socks** – both of whom said they had come along to help their sister. But she thought it was more likely just for a chance to have a sneaky peek at the mystical collar

The group left the animal parliament via the drains, which was the quickest exit to the river while keeping out of sight of humans. They emerged just under a pier where Londoners, *TOURISTS – AND ANIMALS! –* could catch the boat up and down the river.

THE ANIMAL PIER WAS ON THE LEVEL BELOW THE HUMANS' one, and it was a hub of activity. Animals of all shapes and sizes, locals and tourists alike, were waiting to board the next vessel, and busy-looking water voles in uniform were issuing tickets.

Soon after they were ushered on board, **THE HUGE ENGINES OF THE THAMES CLIPPER BOAT ROARED TO LIFE** and they were heading east, leaving Westminster behind.

Toto and her brothers left the ambassador with Sir Fluffypaws in the first-class lounge. **SIR FLUFFYPAWS** was still droning on to **MONSIEUR LAVEUR** that something had to be done about the pigeons.

CREAK

SQUEAK
SQUEAK

'But they are citizens too, *non*?' the French
rat said.

'They are not the same, monsieur,' the old
ginger cat said pompously. 'London hasn't

seen the like since the great horse manure
crisis of 1894 when my great-great-great-
great-great-grandfather was in power, ah
yes, back in the days when cats were really

cats. If I had my way, bring back catscription, **BLAH BLAH BLAH ...'** he droned on.

Tucked into a hidden nook in the front – the bow – of the boat, Toto enjoyed the feel of the breeze in her fur, while Silver and Socks took in the view of the capital from the water.

They sailed past **WATERLOO BRIDGE,** where both sides of the city opened up to give a spectacular view, then under **BLACKFRIARS BRIDGE** and past the famous animal milk bar, **THE SOUR SAUCER.** Before long, the mighty battleship HMS *Belfast* was visible, moored on the south side of the Thames, and on the north side of the river, the **TOWER OF LONDON ITSELF.**

The huge white stone ramparts of the

Tower loomed high above them as the boat pulled up to the bank. The Tower's turrets jutted up into the London sky, almost daring the world to question its authority. As *SILVER* described the view to his sister, her finely tuned whiskers and ears picked up on flying objects and movements everywhere.

'Don't worry, sis,' Silver said, noticing her alertness. 'Nothing to fret about. Quite the opposite – my, what a sight ... *IT'S THE RAVENS.*'

'I told you they were something else.' Socks smiled, gazing in awe.

Tilting her face up to the sky, Toto could just about make out black shadows, swooping, banking and arching in a swarm around the tower. The birds were putting on a display for their visitors that was at once a spectacle and a message.

There was no doubt about who was in charge here.

The human tourists disembarked from a gangway, while the animals had their own exit at the bow of the boat. The ambassador's group congregated by an ominous-looking sign that read: **TRAITORS' GATE**.

'Yikes! Not sure anyone would have liked to be getting off here back in the day – you'd be for the chop!' Socks gulped.

Suddenly, just in front of them, **TWELVE RAVENS** landed expertly in unison, led by an older bird with a **BLACK AND RED SCARF.** It was he who came forward to address them all.

'Ambassador, Home Secretary, welcome to the Tower of London. **MY NAME IS CYRIL CORVUSTON.** I've been the **CHIEF RAVEN** here for the past twenty years. May I introduce to you my elite squadron.'

ATTENTION

At this, the serious-looking birds behind him bowed as one, sending a flutter of air through Toto's whiskers.

Toto and the others were impressed. She might have been a ninja, but Toto knew how hard it would be to move in unison like these birds, and she sensed that their discipline and teamwork must mean they were as well trained as any ninja she'd met.

'It's our sincere honour to host you here, Ambassador. I know you don't have too much time, so if you'll please follow my assistant Edgar, we shall begin.' Cyril nodded to a raven behind him, who led the way into the heart of the Tower. **LARRY AND TOTO FELL IN LINE NEXT TO CYRIL,** who hopped along beside them. Toto had to admit she was pretty intimidated by Cyril's formal tone, but as soon as the rest of the delegation were a few steps ahead he seemed to relax a little bit.

'Larry, my old chum, I have to say, I could have done without this today. I slept so weirdly last night – *I FEEL LIKE I'VE BEEN DRAGGED THROUGH A NEST BACKWARDS!*' the raven confessed.

'You were probably just a little nervous about today going well. Thanks again for accommodating us at such short notice! Your aerobatics were quite the show, most impressive, so you've won them over already. A quick *GLANCE AT THE JEWELS* and Monsieur Laveur and old stuffy whiskers will be more than happy.'

'Yes, I suppose so. I just feel so groggy ... Anyway, delighted that I finally get to meet your prodigy, Toto!' The bird stuck out a wing for Toto to shake.

'Nice to meet you, sir, what a display!' Toto beamed.

'It's Cyril, young lady, and thank you. We like to please the tourists, human and animal alike. A couple of loop-the-loops and they shower us with treats to eat. I'm still full from *LAST NIGHT'S BLOOD BISCUITS!*'

'Urgh!' blurted out Toto, involuntarily. 'Sorry, I don't mean to be rude, but is that a thing?'

'Oh yes, had them for my dinner. Got sent to me as a present from an anonymous admirer, tourist probably, happens a lot. Biscuits dipped in blood are a raven's favourite.'

Just behind Toto, Socks and Silver were laughing at her disgust and licking their chops! Silver's greediness seemed to be rubbing off on his new brother – they liked to eat *anything*!

Cyril chuckled too. 'Now, if you'll excuse me, I'd better make sure our esteemed guests don't get lost. *Squawk!*' He flapped his wings and made off to catch up with the ambassador.

For the next hour or so, the party visited the most fascinating and historical parts of the Tower, including the armoury. 'All the animal arsenal in the world is stored here, from the **BATTLE OF CATGINCOURT** to the elite Napoleonic dog units,' explained Cyril.

But it was obvious what the group really wanted to see, and Cyril didn't disappoint. 'Of course, we save the very best to last,' he said as they reached a big old oak door that led to the top of a turret.

'**OLD TOM'S COLLAR** is the most **SACRED OBJECT** in our kingdom. It was bequeathed by Old Tom himself, the first animal guardian of Britain. His vow to protect our world has now passed down to Larry and Toto.'

While the other animals hung on every word, Sir Fluffypaws was having none of it. It was clear he really wasn't a fan of the ninjas. Rolling his eyes,he interrupted rudely, 'Yes, yes, all fine, can we just see the jewels?'

Cyril, unflustered, continued, 'Only **TWO KEYS EXIST** in the world: this one I keep in my plumage; the other is kept by the current holder of Tom's post, Larry. Without these keys, it is simply impenetrable. Now if you'll follow me.' He opened the door with a flourish and they all climbed the stone stairs beyond.

'Oh my days! **I CAN'T WAIT TO SEE THIS COLLAR, TOTO,**' Socks said as he bounded up excitedly. 'I've only seen it in pictures, but

I know it's so beautiful!'

Silver nudged Toto, as they climbed the stairs, and saw her beam with pride. 'To think, one day you'll be the one holding that key, sis, if those cats back in Italy could see us now!'

After two flights, the party arrived at a landing. Cyril unlocked another door which led to a small circular room, at the centre of which was a velvet curtain.

'Behold!' he announced and drew the velvet curtains to reveal ... *NOTHING!* It was just an empty glass case with its door open.

Everyone gasped. The whiskers on Larry's face drooped and Cyril didn't look too much happier. The two old friends stared in

disbelief at each other, as if to ask the same
question: *HOW COULD THE COLLAR
BE GONE?*

The first animal to regain some composure
was, unfortunately, Sir Wigbert Fluffypaws
the Third.

'**THIS IS AN OUTRAGE!** What do you two have to say for yourselves? You have lost the most precious thing this government owns! Not to mention the embarrassment this has caused us in front of our distinguished guests!' he shouted.

'*Mon ami*, I'm sure there is a reasonable explanation,' the ambassador piped up. He seemed to be trying to defuse the situation.

'**OH, THERE'S AN EXPLANATION ALL RIGHT. ONE OF THESE TWO, OR BOTH OF THEM MORE LIKELY, HAVE STOLEN IT!**'

'That's ridiculous,' interrupted Toto. 'They were both with us the whole time. You can't accuse my boss without some proof!'

'You heard the raven say it himself: "the only two keys in the world! Impenetrable!" So, answer me, missy, what more proof do I need? Who else could have taken them? Or are you telling me your boss is so incompetent he just *let* the collar be stolen?'

Toto hung her head and was silent, not entirely sure what to say.

But next to her, Socks was shaking his paw. 'You old fool! *LARRY'S THE GREATEST CAT THERE'S EVER BEEN IN 10 DOWNING STREET.* No one in their right mind would Adam and Eve what you're saying, so give it a rest, you muppet.'

Not wanting to be outdone by his little brother, but looking slightly confused, Silver rounded off the barrage of insults by saying, 'I'm not a hundred per cent sure what Socksy just said, but, yeah, me too! You muppet!'

'**HOW DARE YOU?**' Sir Fluffypaws' fur was standing on end, he was so angry. 'This will be the end of the Ninja Cats, mark my words. It's clear you're all in on the heist! You've been far too independent and unruly, and now it's come to this. And you, raven, you'll be for the chop as well. Miss Snarlingfoot, arrest them all!'

The room was totally still for a moment; no one was quite sure what to do. Ten Alsatian police dogs were poised to make the arrest, but, confused, they looked to Sheila for orders. She, in turn, looked pleadingly at Larry. The cat, however, looked beaten and just shrugged his shoulders and sat down on the floor.

'**I SAID: ARREST THEM ALL!**'
Fluffypaws screamed.

Sheila reluctantly gave the order to arrest Larry, Cyril, Toto, Silver and Socks.

Toto had to act fast. She was pretty sure she could take all ten of the Alsatians, but she wasn't too keen on fighting her friends and colleagues. She was torn, but then Larry looked up and whispered one word, so quietly that only her super sensitive hearing could make out what he was saying: 'Run!'

At that, she knew what she had to do. Two Alsatians closed in on her, but she had her bearings and could make out the walls of the room and a window ... a window to who knew where, but anywhere was better than here.

Surprising the first dog, she ran towards him and slid between his legs to arrive perfectly under the second, whose tail she grabbed to swing herself towards the wall. Bouncing off it expertly, she grabbed both of her surprised brothers by the scruffs of their necks, and landed on the window ledge.

On the other side of the room, Cyril and Larry were being led away in handcuffs while the rest of the police were closing in on her. Larry looked up and shouted out, '*HOPE LIES UNDER THE MILK TROLLEY!*'

But the three cats didn't have time to work out what he meant – with the dogs closing in, they took the only option available to them and jumped into the unknown.

CHAPTER 3

They hit the icy River Thames hard, the freezing-cold water numbing Toto instantly. Luckily, since her last aquatic adventure at Catstonbury, she been taking lessons from her friend Lutra the otter, and was now a competent swimmer. She actually quite *liked* the water, in fact. The same couldn't be said for her brothers, who she could sense were floundering in the fast-flowing river. Listening over the torrent of water, she could just about make out their voices.

'**HELP!** I can only swim half a length with armbands!' she heard Silver yell.

'Don't worry, I'm coming!' she called.

Swimming powerfully, she cut across the current to where he and Socks were both kicking and spluttering.

'**HOLD ON TO ME. AND DON'T PANIC,**' she told her brothers. Toto knew she'd have to take that advice herself. Yes, she wasn't a bad swimmer, but there was no way she had the strength to keep her head above the water and support her two brothers for long. The ninja knew she had to think of something fast. Breathing slowly, she concentrated on the ripples in the water around her, searching for anything they could grab hold of.

'Over there, sis, a fallen tree!' For once, Silver was way ahead of her. But the tree was in a part of the river that was flowing faster – she'd have one shot to make it or they'd be goners!

She kicked towards the floating trunk, but with her brothers' weight and her freezing body beginning to tire, she started to feel it was hopeless ... They'd never make it. She tried to clear her mind and focus – surely she could do something to give them a chance?

'LINK PAWS AND DON'T LET GO,' she yelled.

With her last ounce of strength, Toto

hurled the two cats through the air. So they formed a kind of **CAT DAISY CHAIN!** It was Silver who landed on the trunk of the old oak and, scrambling up, he managed to drag Socks and then Toto on to the tree and to safety. Exhausted, they all lay still for a moment, bewildered and stunned, and tried to work out what had just happened.

TOTO WAS CONFUSED, uncertain and even a little angry with her boss. *SURELY HE COULDN'T BE GUILTY OF STEALING OLD TOM'S COLLAR,* but who else apart from him and Cyril had a key? And it was more than that. He had looked so defeated ... why wouldn't he fight back if he was innocent? Toto tried to shake that thought – this was *LARRY*. He was a ninja and her friend. There had to be another reason for the way he'd acted.

Toto's thoughts were interrupted by Socks. 'What was that thing Larry said before we escaped? "Hope lies under the milk trolley"? I haven't a scooby what that could mean. Do you, sis?'

Toto just shook her head. Without her

mentor, she didn't even know where to start! As they were all pondering this, the large trunk gently came to rest at the side of the riverbank. The cats all looked up; they were now far from the heart of the city, where the river was quieter, and the banks were lined with bright green grass. If it wasn't for the predicament they found themselves in, the beach they had been washed up on would be a perfect place for a picnic. Which was apt, because as they looked around, they saw a human child's toy boat moored up and a familiar face enjoying just that.

'WELL I SAY, THIS IS A WONDERFUL SURPRISE! DID YOU PLAN IT? CARE FOR AN EGG SANDWICH?'

Lying on the beach by the river bank, book

in hand, a picnic basket full of sandwiches, roast chicken and pork pies by his side (Silver couldn't help but lick his lips) and a fishing rod dug into the sand, their cat-rat pal was enjoying a VERY different day from the one the cats were having.

'*CATFACE!*' His friends crowded around and had a much-needed hug.

'*WHAT ARE YOU DOING HERE?*' Toto asked.

'I could ask you the same thing! It's my day off, remember? Although the fishing's not going too well – I know half of these fish, so it feels terrible catching them, much less eating them!'

'Afternoon, Catface, smashing day,' a passing perch called as it surfaced.

'Oh, hello, Priscilla!' Catface waved. 'See? Hopeless. Anyway, my furry friends, from the looks on your faces, something bad has happened.'

After the cats had filled him in on the recent events (and Silver had helped himself to a few egg sandwiches), the older, wise rodent sat on the side of his boat and pondered what to do.

'Well, I can't believe that Larry would steal anything, much less Old Tom's Collar. Cyril, too, he's as loyal as they come. They must be being framed for this – someone has set them up,' he concluded firmly.

'Other than its value, what do you know about the collar?' asked Silver.

'Well, much of it is just myth, really, but for us rats the collar has a chequered history. **KING RODERICK THE FILTHY DIRTY WAS THE ORIGINAL HOLDER OF THE COLLAR.** Ghastly rat, wanted to wipe out all other animals and humans with a plague! No self-respecting rat nowadays would hear of such a thing. After old Tom bested Roderick in combat, the ownership of the collar passed to him. Legend has it that whoever holds the collar has power, and holds sway over all of the rat population, and oddly the pigeons, too. Tom, being a decent sort, didn't want a part in any of that old nonsense and decided to put it under lock and key in the Tower. Which is where it's been ever since. It makes no sense for Larry or Cyril to steal it, especially since relations between cats and rats are at an all-time high. I'm sorry, that's all I know. And what on earth Larry meant by "Hope lies under the milk trolley!" is anyone's guess. Is he off his rocker?'

"Ere, Catface.' The party turned to see Socks sitting on the gunwale of the boat, looking into the distance. 'Who's the one person who knows more about London and its history than anyone else, even you?'

'By Jove, you might be on to something, young Socks. **MATILDA!** Owner of the **RAGDOLL BOOK EMPORIUM.** She's an old ragdoll cat, and her bookshop has the world's best selection of history books. If anyone can help us get to the bottom of this, she can. Right, get on board, cats, and brace yourselves,' he said as he put on a ship captain's hat. 'I'm about to break the river speed limit.'

Catface powered up the motorboat and sailed like a rat possessed back to central London. They were soon moored up on the north side of the Thames, by a storm drain that Catface was sure would take them to a manhole right by the bookshop.

WHOOSH

'*CATS, WE MUST BE CAREFUL,*' Catface instructed once they reached the ladder that would take them up to ground level. 'When we we're in central London in broad daylight we must be fast, and try not to be spotted. Humans aren't the greatest fans of rats, and you're all still on the run, so look out for any police dogs. Ready? Let's move.'

One by one the gang made their way up the ladder. At the top, Catface lifted the manhole a little and peeked out. 'I think the coast is clear,' he whispered. He quickly **FLIPPED THE LID** and leaped out to run to the safety of the cat flap which served as the **ENTRANCE TO MATILDA'S SHOP**. The rest of the gang followed as fast as they could and made it safely across without being seen.

THE RAGDOLL BOOK EMPORIUM

had stood on the same site for centuries, under an alley of human bookshops near St Martin's Lane in central London. Matilda had run the store for longer than anyone could remember. Old, dusty, weighty books were piled high from floor to ceiling, looking like they could **COME CRASHING DOWN AT ANY MOMENT.** They were stored on interconnected shelves that cats could jump up to, to find their chosen reads. Shards of light shone through a pavement grate on the street above, warming the room. There were comfy sofas in every corner for animals to read on (but, more likely, to nap on!).

'**AH, YOUNG CATFACE, AND MASTER SOCKS.**' The ancient feline smiled as she shuffled towards them. 'Good to see you again. I hope you're both still reading every evening. And THIS must be the **LEGENDARY NINJA CAT** I have heard so much about.' Matilda clasped her paws together and came forward into the light. 'And you must be her brother, I presume, the **COURAGEOUS SILVER**.'

Matilda was a cream cat with a wise face and kind eyes peering out from behind half-rim glasses. She was dressed in a crimson housecoat. Toto got the sense just from her voice that Matilda was a cat who could be trusted, and hopefully give them the knowledge they needed.

'Matilda, we don't have a moment to lose,' the little ninja said. 'What books do you have about *RODERICK THE FILTHY DIRTY AND OLD TOM'S COLLAR?'*

'Old Tom's Collar? Blimey, no one's asked about that for a while ... It's mostly tourists who are about to visit the Tower and I sell them this.' She rustled around on the shelves behind her then held out a book, which Silver grabbed.

'Catface, is this by you?' he blurted. 'It says: *My London* by Alexandre Rattinoff the Thirty-third.'

'Oh, crikey, forgot all about that. I published it just after I qualified as a London guide. It was a big hit, even if I do say so myself, but sadly it won't tell us anything we don't already know.'

'There might be one other, but I haven't

seen it for ages. I think it's down in the basement ... wait here.' Matilda disappeared down some creaky wooden stairs for a few moments before reappearing with a **MASSIVE, DUSTY BOOK.** *'London's Legends* by Catonious Purrstein, written in 1869. If there's anything about Old Tom and the collar, it will be in there. You lot get reading and I'll get the stove on. Hot chocolate and cheese sandwiches all round?'

'Well, we are in quite a rush—' Toto started to say but was interrupted by Catface.

'We'd love some! Seriously, Toto, this might be an emergency, but you HAVE to try Matilda's cheese sandwiches: half Cheddar, half Double Gloucester, with just the slightest hint of Brie ... *C'est magnifique!*'

'**WOO HOO!** And suddenly the day's not looking so bad,' said Silver, trying to lighten the mood.

But Toto still felt worried. *How on earth can we find what we need in this huge book, and in time to save Larry?*

But it wasn't long before the wise old cat returned with the tray of food and drink, and the kittens quickly tucked in as she cracked open the ancient book. 'Now, Old Tom's Collar,' Matilda muttered to herself, as she leafed through pages. 'Here we are: "*THE LEGEND OF OLD TOM'S COLLAR IS A STORY OF BRAVERY, SACRIFICE AND HONESTY. THE EVIL RAT KING RODERICK THE FILTHY DIRTY POSSESSED A COLLAR SO POWERFUL ...*" Yadda, yadda, you know all this ... Hmm. "He fled and was never seen again, but vowed reven—"'

'But he can't be back to take revenge, he'd be more than six hundred years old!' Toto interrupted.

'Wait, there's more,' Matilda continued. '"After the battle, to keep all animals and humans safe, Tom founded The Honourable Guild of Feline Guardians, which later joined together with the Ancient Order of International Ninja Cats!"'

'So Old Tom was *definitely* a ninja!' Silver said excitedly.

Matilda read on. '"Fearing the collar could one day fall into the wrong hands, Tom broke it into two separate bands."'

'**WHAT?!**' the gang said in disbelief.

'**THERE ARE TWO PIECES?**' said Toto.

'Yes, it says here, one band of sapphires, which is the band that was in the Tower, and the second, buried by Tom somewhere in London, is a band of diamonds, the location of which is hidden in a riddle held by Tom's heir. **THE SECOND BAND CAN ONLY BE FOUND IF HE OR SHE CAN SOLVE THE RIDDLE WRITTEN ON THE PARCHMENT. THEN THE TWO BANDS CAN BE RECONNECTED TO ENABLE WHOEVER HOLDS THE COLLAR TO COMMAND EVERY RAT AND PIGEON IN THE COUNTRY ...'**

Matilda sat back and took off her glasses at the terrible thought.

'How many rats are there in the UK now?' asked Toto.

'Ten and a half million on the last census.' Catface gulped. 'And we are a superstitious lot. Who knows **IF THE COLLAR REALLY HOLDS ANY MAGICAL POWER** – but the myth is powerful enough alone since we rats are easily led. We've been so badly persecuted down the years that if word gets out then whoever owns this collar will have huge public support.'

Catface paced up and down for a few moments and suddenly clicked his claws.

'I've got it – allow me a **"EUREKA"**! But we have to act fast. The one person who knows where that riddle is kept is Larry, and there's only one way I know of getting him released from the Tower. We have to go to the highest court in the land and petition for his release.

CATS,
 WE ARE OFF
  TO SEE THE CORGIS OF
   BUCKINGHAM PALACE!'

CHAPTER 4

The gang thanked Matilda and bid her farewell. **'GREATEST CHEESE SANDWICH EVER!'** shouted Silver as they left.

They scurried across the pavement to the manhole that would bring them back to subterranean London. From there Catface said they could make it to Buckingham Palace pretty quickly. As they neared the manhole, however, they heard a shout: **'STOP IN THE NAME OF THE LAW!'**

'YIKES!' screamed Catface as he shot six feet up in the air in surprise. 'Cats, get below ground! NOW!'

The cats ran for cover, but not before they glanced over their shoulders to see three scary-looking police dogs chasing them with teeth bared. One by one, they dropped down into the sewers, with Catface holding the lid for them. Just as the dogs reached the manhole, Catface landed next to the cats, the cover clanking tightly shut behind him.

'Phew,' he said, 'that was close! Still I think we're saf— **OH FOR GOODNESS' SAKE!** You don't even have retractable claws; how did you manage that?' he shouted at the dogs, who had somehow got the manhole cover open with their teeth and were about to drop down into the sewer to give chase.

'Guys, those teeth look awfully big.' Socks gulped. 'What's the plan?'

'Long term: give me a minute,' replied Toto. **'*SHORT TERM: RUUUNNN!*'**

The gang set off with the ginormous dogs in pursuit. Toto probably could have fought the dogs, but she couldn't bear the thought of disobeying Larry. He hadn't wanted her to *attack* the dogs at the Tower, he'd wanted her to *run*. And it seemed like a sensible idea to keep on the right side of the law, especially when she was trying to prove their innocence!

But the dogs were closing in fast. 'Catface, you need to come up with something – I mustn't fight them!' Toto yelped.

'Think, old man, think ...' Catface muttered to himself in response, before clicking his claws, picking up a rusty metal rod from the floor and banging on the pipes that ran along the top of the sewer. **'KITTENS, FOLLOW ME!'**

'I know it seems weird,' Toto told her brothers, 'as usual. But he must know what he's doing, so follow him!'

'On my count, dive into the small tunnel coming up on the right,' Catface instructed. 'Three ... two ... one!'

THE CATS ALL LANDED IN A HEAP IN THE TUNNEL.

'This isn't a plan!' cried Silver. 'Now they'll definitely get u—'

Before he could finish his sentence a torrent of water rushed past in the main tunnel, carrying with it the surprised police dogs, who howled as they were washed away.

'I TOLD YOU!' A gleeful Catface clapped his hands and danced on the spot.

'How did you…?' Toto asked in disbelief at her wise friend.

'Oh, it's a code a bit like Morse that I invented with Matilda a long time ago, back when I wasn't welcome in my dad's kingdom of Ratborough. If I was in trouble near here, I'd bang on the pipes, take cover and she'd do the rest. And by "the rest", I mean she'd flush her human's toilet, which comes right down this tunnel, washing away anything in its path. I do hope that water was clean!'

'Will they be OK? They were only doing their jobs,' asked a concerned Toto.

'They'll be fine, just a bit soggy, and two miles away! Now, my friends, there's not moment to lose – we must make haste.'

The rest of the journey to the palace went smoothly and before long the sewers started to get busier and grander, with very important and regal-looking animals going to and fro. There were fancy shops tucked into the sides of the tunnels, selling all kinds of clothing and food. After a while they reached a huge dark wooden entrance with **'The Animal Law Courts'** written above it.

Catface turned to his friends. 'Right under Buckingham Palace – would you believe it? OK, I know a couple of ferrets that act as the clerks for the corgis. Decent types, they should be able to get me in front of a judge pretty quickly. You three had better make yourself scarce – you're all wanted, remember. *TRY TUCKING YOURSELVES OUT OF SIGHT* down one of the side tunnels and keep a lookout for me.'

But as Catface scurried inside, Socks declared that he had a better idea. 'Come on, you two. I once did a bit of spying on a gangster case with the Battersea Bruisers round 'ere. There's a nice little nook we can squeeze into up this way so we can listen in to what's 'appenin.'

They climbed up through a small tunnel to the side of the court's entrance, then up a rusted ladder to a little ledge that was almost invisible from the ground. Socks wiped away some muck from the wall to reveal a crack that he and Silver could peek through, while Toto leaned her ear close.

A SNOOTY FERRET in a cape was just addressing the court: '*ALL RISE, THE SUPREME COURT IS NOW IN SESSION, THE*

HONOURABLE JUDGE LADY ANGHARAD
OF PEMBROKE PRESIDING.'

The whole court stood as a corgi in red dress robes shuffled in to take her seat.

The ferret continued, 'Your Honour, today's case is somewhat different from the schedule. It's a last-minute addition, a plea.'

'**WHAT?**' the confused corgi exclaimed in a booming Welsh accent, looking up from her papers. 'I have a busy enough morning as it is. I have to hear a case of a missing goldfish, the penguins from the zoo are due to settle a fish dispute, and I've got two peregrine falcons suing each other over hunting rights in Hyde Park. I don't have time for an extra plea!'

'Err, yes, Your Honour,' the ferret answered nervously, 'but I think you'll agree that it is

rather important. Today's case is Mr Cyril the raven and Mr Larry the cat vs the Crown. Making a plea on behalf of the defendant is Alexandre Rattinoff the Thirty-third.'

THE COURT GASPED.

'Catface?' The corgi's frosty demeanour evaporated in a flash. 'My dear boy! *LARRY ARRESTED?* What on earth is going on?'

It was clear, like most animals the cats encountered, that she knew Catface already.

'Is there anyone he hasn't met?' Toto muttered to her brothers, smiling, as they watched proceedings from their vantage.

'He certainly looks the part,' said Silver, going on to explain to his sister that somehow their friend had found some lawyer's robes and a wig!

Lady Angharad addressed the court. 'Now, Catface, my boy, why don't you tell me what all this is about, and we'll see if we can't get all this sorted, eh?'

Catface then proceeded, in true showman style, to win over both Lady Angharad and the rest of the court as he told the whole story of the missing jewels.

'So, you see, Your Honour,' he concluded, 'while it's true the **JEWELS ARE MISSING,** there isn't a scrap of evidence, witness accounts or motive to convict Larry and Cyril. In fact, one might argue they are vital to the safe return of these sacred jewels ... The defence rests.'

Having exhausted himself, Catface took off his glasses ('He doesn't even wear glasses!'

whispered Silver) and slumped into his chair.

The court erupted in applause, with every animal on their feet.

'Order, ORDER!' a clearly impressed Lady Angharad shouted and the court fell silent. All eyes turned to her. 'Catface, you present a very good defence for your friends, and while the court admits there are still questions to be answered about the whereabouts of Old Tom's Collar, it is clear to the court that both Larry and Cyril are innocent until proven guilty, so they should be released forthwith and—'

'STOP THIS IMMEDIATELY!'

All eyes turned to the back of the court, where an angry **SIR FLUFFYPAWS STOOD, HUFFING AND PUFFING.** He had clearly been informed about the plea and had run to the court at great speed.

'THIS COURT IS A SHAM! A KANGAROO COURT!'

'Actually, Home Secretary, the kangaroos are in the courtroom next door; I believe they're involved in a case involving the theft of eucalyptus leaves by a gang of koalas,' the sheepish-looking ferret said with a wince.

'**IT'S A FIGURE OF SPEECH, YOU IDIOT!**
It means this whole procedure is a farce. I locked Larry and Cyril up with the authority invested in me by the animal parliament, and there is no way they should be released. They are a threat to the safety of this nation, and this cat ... rat ... *thing*' – Sir Fluffypaws rounded on Catface – 'isn't even a qualified lawyer!'

'Oh crumbs,' muttered Catface under his breath.

The court gasped again.

'Catface, is this true?' Lady Angharad demanded of her friend.

'Weeeellll, technically ... I mean, I did study law but a week before graduation I got an offer to be a ship's cat/rat on a boat carrying corned beef to Brazil, and my sense of adventure got the better of me ... sorry. But the facts still remain! Larry and Cyril are innocent.'

'If you grant them freedom I'll have this court stripped of its authority by nightfall,' boomed the home secretary.

Lady Angharad sighed heavily and addressed the court. 'Much as it would please the court to grant Larry and Cyril their freedom, sadly, the home secretary is correct – Catface isn't actually a lawyer. Until we can have a full trial to prove their INNOCENCE,' she said, glaring at Fluffypaws, 'or their guilt, the court has no choice. Case dismissed.' She banged her gavel wearily.

'**HUZZAH,**' Fluffypaws shouted arrogantly and, giving Catface a contemptuous stare, stomped out of the court followed by his staff.

Catface, dejected, shuffled his papers and left too. The cats leaped to the floor of the tunnel to go and meet him.

'Sorry, guys,' Catface said, and slumped up against the wall next to the courthouse, almost in tears. 'I knew I should have stuck around to finish my law degree ... but that trip to Brazil was brilliant.'

'Is there anything you haven't done?' asked Silver.

'Oh, you know, I've dabbled in all sorts of bits and bobs ... no help today, mind. Well, I'm out of ideas – what do you three think?'

Toto took control. 'Time for Plan B. There are two things we have to do. One, get to the bottom of that odd clue Larry gave us: "Hope lies under the milk trolley". If we're looking for a clue, where would be the one place Larry knows better than anywhere else, and where there's also a magnificent milk trolley?'

'His office, below 10 Downing Street!' replied Silver. '*Mamma mia*! Why didn't we think of it before? I still have dreams about that milk trolley.'

'Snap out of it, brother,' Toto said, clicking her claws.

'Sorry ... not sorry,' Silver muttered.

'Catface, you get over there and see if you can see what's hidden below Larry's milk trolley.'

'Good idea,' her friend replied. 'What's the second thing?'

'Something I swore in my ninja vows I would never do,' Toto said with a glint in her eye. 'I'm going to break the law. **WE'RE BUSTING LARRY AND CYRIL OUT!**'

CHAPTER 5

The journey back to the Tower of London via the sewers passed without incident. Soon, Toto, Silver and Socks found themselves on the bank of the south side of the Thames, looking over the water to the Tower.

Socks had run off for ten minutes or so, saying he had to go and get something important, but had just returned.

THE TOWER WAS A FOREBODING SIGHT. The ravens circled around one of the turrets with intimidating, awesome prowess.

'That turret there must be where they are holding Larry and Cyril,' said Socks as he described the scene to Toto, before lowering a pair of binoculars and passing them over to his brother.

'Where did you find these?' asked Silver.

'**MY MATE DAVE.** He's a crow who runs a store not far from here. Anything you need, Dave can get it for you, no questions asked, if you know what I mean.'

'I don't want to know what you mean! But never mind that for now. This isn't going to be a walk in the park; those ravens are impressive, and we're used to *arresting* criminals, not breaking them out,' said Toto.

'Chill, sis! When I went to borrow these binoculars, I had a chat with Dave about our Barney Rubble—'

'That means 'trouble' in London code, Toto, remember?' Silver whispered.

'—and he sorted us out with this!' Socks smiled triumphantly as he produced a sleek black drone from behind his back. 'It's the latest technology; Dave says it can fly anywhere. So, here's my plan: Silver, you take the controls. I jump on, you fly me over to the Tower, I break into the cell, Cyril flies out, Larry gets on board the drone, then we whisk him back here before the ravens are any the wiser. *AND WE ARE BACK IN THE*

GAME! EASY! HIGH FIVE!' He produced his paw and while his brother and sister indulged him, Toto was certain this would be anything but *easy*.

'I 'VE GOT A GREAT FEELING ABOUT THIS!' the little kitten shouted over the noise as he mounted the drone and put on some flying goggles. 'Aim for that window at the top of the nearest turret. I reckon there's a gap of about fifteen seconds between raven patrols – that's the time to get me in and out. Roger?'

'Roger,' replied Silver as he took control of the drone and started to pilot it across the Thames.

'Piece of cake, this, sis. Genius idea from the little fella.' Silver beamed.

The drone was now well over halfway to the Tower. Silver was steering it just above the water of the Thames and out of sight of the ravens. As it got closer, Silver slowed down and waited for Socks to give him the signal ... then, just as predicted, a squadron of ravens swooped by the turret and flew out of sight. Socks waved his paw, and Silver powered up the drone, so it shot high into the air to hover just outside the window where Larry and Cyril were being held.

'*TAXI FOR MR LARRY?*' Socks said with a grin as he got to the window.

Before Larry even had a chance to get to his feet and ask what young Socks was doing thirty metres above ground, he and the drone disappeared from view.

'Uh-oh,' said Silver on the other side of the river. '*THE RAVENS ARE BACK.*'

Although Toto couldn't see them, she could certainly hear the noise they were making, and it didn't bode well.

The flock of ravens, led by Cyril's assistant

Edgar, all look turns attacking the drone and poor Socks, who could do nothing but hang on for dear life as they pecked and swung their razor-sharp beaks and talons in his direction.

'*GIVE OVER! HEY, I WAS JUST TAKING A JOY RIDE AND GOT LOST!*'

Back on the south side of the river, Silver was doing his best to get his little brother out of trouble. But with all the attacks on the drone, it wasn't responding, and he was losing power and control. Lurching up and down and back and forth, the drone slowly made its spluttering way back to the bank. As soon as they realised it posed no more threat, the

pursuing ravens regrouped and went back into formation, patrolling around the turret.

Just as Socks was about to make it back on to dry land, smoke started coming out of it the drone. It gave up the ghost and dropped like a stone into the icy Thames.

'ARRRGGHH! TWICE IN A DAY!'

Socks cried as he plunged into the river

again. Luckily, he was right by the river side, and so could swim easily to the concrete embankment, where his brother and sister hauled him out. Although they knew how serious the situation was, they couldn't help but laugh. Socks was wet through, and he grimaced as he spat out a mouthful of Thames water, which had a tiny fish in it.

'Cor, they don't call them "an unkindness of ravens" for nothing. Dave the crow is going to kill me; I was supposed to return that drone... Right. Any other ideas? Because I'm all out!'

'I think I might have one,' Toto said, as she cuddled her little brother to warm him up. 'But it's a long shot, and almost certainly won't work.'

'Excellent!' replied Silver. 'Those types of ideas are our speciality!'

'You want me to what?' said Mary the seagull, shaking her head. 'No, absolutely not. Are you out of your mind? As plans go this is pretty much the most hare-brained thing I've ever heard, and that includes all of Catface's ideas ... all of them.'

In Toto's mind, the idea was simple, if unlikely. **BUT SHE HAD TO GET LARRY OUT OF THAT CELL,** and she was prepared to try anything. She needed wings and **MARY, THE QUEEN OF LONDON'S SEAGULLS,** was one of the best flyers in the business and a trusted ally of the cats. Toto thought that if they could disguise Mary to look like a raven, then, if they picked their moment right, they could get in and out to rescue Larry and Cyril with the ravens being none the wiser.

'*JUST HOW AM I SUPPOSED TO PASS FOR A RAVEN?* It may have escaped your notice that I am a seagull. Our feathers are entirely different colours!'

'Which is where this fine gent comes in. May we present *DAVE THE CROW*,' Socks said with a flourish.

'*DELIGHTED TO MAKE YOUR ACQUAINTANCE*,' said Dave, as he hopped out from behind a nearby wheelie bin. He was an old and unkempt crow, wearing a trilby hat and a sheepskin jacket.

'Charmed, I'm sure,' replied Mary, 'but I still don't follow.'

Silver stepped in to explain. 'Dave is a fine upstanding citizen and good friend of little Socks here, and when he heard of our predicament, he was only too happy to come and help.'

Socks gave his best puppy-eyed look (which is no mean feat when you're a cat) and continued, 'For a VERY small price ... very small, Dave has agreed we can **PLUCK HIS BEAUTIFUL FEATHERS** then stick them on to you, and **YOU CAN PASS FOR A RAVEN!**'

'I see, and what does Dave want for such a selfless act?' Mary asked, rolling her eyes.

'Half your take of fish from one day at Billingsgate Fish Market?' Silver winced.

'**THAT'S A FORTUNE!**' Mary squawked. 'I'm the biggest fish supplier for animals in all of London.'

'Well, feathers take a good long time to grow back, y'know. I'll be needing to buy a warm jumper. Oh, and they owe me for that drone they ruined.' Dave smiled.

'You cats are going to bankrupt me, but for Larry I'll do it.' Mary shook her head in resignation, then turned to the crow. 'Dave, I'm not going to lie, this is going to hurt you and me both!'

'Awwwwwoooooo, not so hard!' the old crow cried as the last of the feathers was plucked from him. Poor Dave did look a little bare, but with all that fish coming his way he was more than happy. Mary, on the other hand, looked like she could pass for a raven ... *just*.

'We don't need you to look like a raven up close, just from afar. If we get stopped we are almost certainly rumbled, so just

try to fly like a raven so they don't come to investigate,' Toto said as she tucked herself under Mary's plumage. 'When we get there, I'll jump off on to the window ledge of the cell, and break Larry out, then you fly like the wind and get us out of there.'

'You AND Larry? You'll be a bit heavy. But I'll do my best,' the huge gull said as she took a waddling run-up and launched into the air.

MARY MADE STRAIGHT FOR THE TURRET where Larry and Cyril were being held. They judged the changeover of the raven squadrons just right this time and, in no time, they got to the window ledge of the cell. Toto jumped off ready to break out her boss. Just as she was about to call out to him, though, she heard a curt squawk followed by a military-sounding: **'WHO GOES THERE?'** One of the ravens had returned.

Toto pushed herself tightly against the window so she was hidden from the raven's view. Toto thought fast and whispered, 'Repeat after me, Mary: I'm from catering, just delivering the prisoners' dinner.'

Mary quickly repeated the line, but the raven eyed her suspiciously and said, 'What are the traitors having?'

'Err,' Mary stalled, then something came to her. **'*ROTTEN FISH!*'** And she produced a stinky mackerel head from under her wing.

'Phowarrr ... Awful, rather them than me! Still, no less than a traitor deserves. Well, I'm off on patrols – had a little cat on a drone try to come over here earlier. We gave him what for, ha!' And with that the raven took off in the opposite direction.

'Where did you get that fish head?' asked Toto.

'*ALWAYS GOOD TO HAVE A SNACK IN AN EMERGENCY!* That raven wasn't one of their most intelligent recruits, was he?' Mary laughed. **'NOW, HOW ABOUT WE FREE YOUR BOSS AND GET OUT OF HERE?'**

The rusted iron bars that had been in place for centuries were no match for Toto, and with a swift kick she was inside the cell.

The floor was covered in straw, with a couple of old beds on either side. Sitting at each end, clearly tired but pleasantly surprised, were **LARRY AND CYRIL.**

'Come on, boss, time to get you out of here and clear your name,' Toto said with a smile.

Larry shot up and turned to Cyril. 'Coming, old friend?'

'No, I must stay here,' replied the raven. 'If I run I'll never get my job back. But go, Larry, and **PROVE US BOTH INNOCENT.'**

'**YOU BET,**' Larry replied, and he and Toto climbed on to Mary's back and were gone into the London sky.

'Just one thing, boss,' Toto shouted against the wind. '"Hope lies under the milk trolley." Really? You could have been a bit more obvious.'

'I didn't want to give the game away … I thought with the dairy reference it would be easy enough for Silver. Was I right?'

'Yes, well, no … but we got there in the end. When you put it like that, it does make perfect sense. But why didn't you try to escape with us in the first place?'

'I know it seems silly, but I couldn't bear to look like I was trying to be above the law. Fluffypaws is always accusing us ninjas of doing just that and it's infuriating. But as soon as I was locked up, I realised I'd made a mistake. We need to all be together, working as a team to solve this. The risks are too high for my pride to get in the way. You did well to get me out, Toto!'

Mary was soon scooping up Toto's brothers by their collars to fly them all to Downing Street where they could start to clear Larry's name and get to the bottom of this mystery once and for all.

As Toto felt the wind come off the river and blow through her fur, she realised that **EVEN THOUGH THEY WERE ON THE RUN, SHE'D NEVER BEEN MORE EXCITED.**

CHAPTER 6

'CARRYING FOUR CATS! My poor back is killing, me, plus I've lost half a day's take from Billingsgate AND it'll take me ages to get these smelly crow feathers out of my plumage. Toto, you owe me. Next time you need a favour, call someone else,' Mary moaned as she dropped the four cats in the safety of some bushes near

10 DOWNING STREET. (Though she gave Toto a friendly hug goodbye to show she wasn't too annoyed.)

'Good luck, you lot – get that collar back safe and sound. I'm off for some much-needed fish and chips and a steam bath … *LAAVELY!*' She flapped her wings and was off.

'So, what's the plan, boss? How do we get into your office without being seen?' Toto asked.

'It's not going to be easy, but that air conditioning vent over there should lead directly to a pipe above my office. We'll have to be as quiet as mice, ones that aren't being chased by cats. I'll go first. Toto, you go at the back. Remember, we are all wanted now, so the CIA will be all over the building in case we turn up.'

LARRY SPRINTED, unseen, from the bushes to the vent opening.

The hope now was that they could solve the riddle to find the other part of the collar before the thief did, and clear Larry's name once and for all.

The air conditioning pipes were a pretty tight squeeze and a couple of times they had to freeze when they saw police dogs on patrol through the vents. But ten minutes later they were directly over Larry's office. The head ninja silently removed the vent and slipped down on to his desk, ushering the others down behind him. It was clear all was not right: the place was a scene of chaos. Somebody had clearly turned the place upside down looking for the clue.

Larry moved papers and furniture around as quietly as possible. He shifted the milk trolley to reveal an opened and empty safe. **'BLAST! IT'S GONE.'**

For a second the gang of four stood still, not quite knowing their next move. But then they heard something stirring in the corner

of the room, where an upturned armchair was covered with old papers and maps. Instinctively, **LARRY AND TOTO** pushed the two brothers behind them and took up a **NINJA FIGHTING STANCE.**

'OH, MY HEAD,' a very groggy Catface groaned, as he got to his feet.

'What happened?' asked Toto, rushing over to help him up.

'It was all going swimmingly to start with. I was able to charm my way through security – said I was looking for some papers to help with your case, Larry.' Catface winked conspiratorially. **'AS SOON AS I WAS IN HERE, I MADE STRAIGHT FOR THE MILK TROLLEY AND CRACKED OPEN THE SAFE.'**

The cats looked at him in surprise.

'Don't be so surprised! I learned from the best: Abbe the eel, Dutch guy, master safe cracker. You arrested him last year, Toto? Anyway, I found the parchment and was just about to solve the riddle, when—'

'When what?' the cats asked with bated breath.

'When I got clocked over the head by some rotter. I only came to just now.'

'Which means **WHOEVER KNOCKED YOU OUT NOW HAS THE RIDDLE.** If they can crack that they can reunite the two collars and then ... rat domination,' said Toto with a grimace.

'Yes, rather bad luck, I'm afraid. But there is one bit of silver lining: I can remember the riddle! See, learning songs for all those gigs has been good for something.' Catface cleared his throat then recited:

'I lie below where horses tread,

Before the carts and wheels go red,

In water low, but hill so high,

Where the city kisses the sky.

You'll find me safe and buried there,

Above London's smoke-filled air.

So, take a breath and you will find

The treasure to control rats' minds.'

Toto shrugged and Silver looked blank. **'DON'T ASK US ... WE'RE ITALIAN!'**

Larry, Catface and Socks all started pacing the room while Silver helped himself to a nice Jersey milk from Larry's famous drinks trolley. It was the little Battersea cat who piped up first.

'"Water low, but hill so high". Where are there ponds on a hill in London ... Hampstead Heath? But the ponds have no relation to horses; that can't be it.'

'I know one that does!' Catface interjected. **'WHITESTONE POND.** It's right at the top of the hill at Hampstead. In olden times it was called Horse Pond, because the horses drank and rested and the carts' iron wheels that they were pulling were cooled off in the water.'

'Cooled off?' asked Toto

'Yes, you see, as the carts got to the top of the hill the metal in the wheels got hot and expanded, making it harder to use the brakes. So, they were dunked in the pond before they went down the hill on the other side, meaning the brakes would work. Remember the line in the riddle: 'London's smoke-filled air'? Well, Hampstead used to be a village, just outside the grimy city. It all makes sense. The second part of Old Tom's Collar is at the bottom of that pond, I'm sure of it. We need to get to Hampstead – fast.'

Just as the party was about to climb back up into the pipes, ***THE DOOR BURST OPEN*** and in came several ***POLICE DOGS: SOME***

ROTTWEILERS, SOME ALSATIANS, ALL LOOKING SERIOUS.

The lead dog piped up. 'Sorry, Larry, Toto, we have ORDERS TO ARREST YOU ON SIGHT. Oh, and you, Catface, for impersonating a lawyer, apparently.'

'Oh, come on, that was nothing, just a misunderstanding!'

'Well, we still have to take you all in, so will you come quietly, or is this going to get messy?'

Larry and Toto moved silently into position in front of the others. Toto had already broken the law once today – she could hardly believe she was about to do it again.

'You really don't have to do this,' the older cat implored. 'The country is at risk and we need to—'

'That's enough! Dogs, arrest them,' came the answer.

'THEN WE TRULY ARE SORRY.' LARRY SIGHED. 'TOTO, LET'S GET TO WORK.'

The next thirty seconds went by in a blur, as Catface, Silver and Socks had a front row seat to watch in awe as the squadron of police dogs were soundly and swiftly dispatched by a **DISPLAY OF NINJA AWESOMENESS.**

Larry was incredible – even Toto had never experienced him like this. A roundhouse kick took out three police dogs in one go. He **DUCKED AND DODGED** as the lead police dog, who was by far the toughest of the mob, aimed punch after punch at him but to no avail. The police chief just couldn't lay a paw

on Larry, who, with his paws behind his back, frustrated the huge dog. Then, crouching down, he sprang at the canine, aiming a kick into his midriff that sent him crashing into a filing cabinet.

For her part, Toto was easily dispatching her fair share of attackers, but like Larry she was reluctant to do any real harm. These were animals that worked for her friend Sheila – normally they'd be on the same team! **FOR EACH PUNCH OR KICK, BOTH LARRY AND TOTO WERE HUGELY APOLOGETIC.**

'SORRY!'

BAM!

'I DO BEG YOUR PARDON!'

WHACK!

It might have been over in seconds, but it was probably the politest cat fight in history!

The last of the assailants was thrown across the room and landed at the feet of Silver, who had been watching the whole thing while tucking into Larry's supply of top-notch Jersey milk. With the ornate jug now empty, Silver smashed it on the huge dog's head. 'Yeah! Get some! Nice work, boss, sis – we did a great job here.'

His sister shook her head and smiled. 'Yeah, great work, brother.'

'Sorry about the jug, Larry.' Silver smiled sheepishly.

'Oh, don't worry about that. It was a Christmas present from old Fluffypaws ... I never liked it. OK, cats, there's not a moment to lose. Whoever found the riddle will be ahead of us. *LET'S GET TO HAMPSTEAD AND THAT POND NOW!'*

CHAPTER 7

IT WAS NIGHTFALL by the time the gang arrived in Hampstead. They were still on the run, so getting to the surface there had to be done on foot via the sewers. Luckily Catface knew the way, and they ran like the wind, so they were still hopeful of finding the collar before the thief.

Just like it had done six hundred years

before, **THE MOON LIT UP THE POND** and a gentle breeze rippled across it. The cats hid for a moment in a nearby bush, but nothing was stirring. Luckily, it looked like they'd got there first, so they cracked a plan.

'Since my lessons with Lutra the otter, I can hold my breath for ages. **I'LL BE THE ONE TO DIVE DOWN –** that OK, boss?' Toto asked Larry.

'Good plan, Toto, but you'll need someone to go with you to help **UNCOVER THAT BOX.** I'll come too.'

'**WAIT A MINUTE.' SILVER GULPED.** 'If the thief did crack that riddle and turns up, we need someone to fight them off. The three of us' – he gestured to Catface and Socks – 'might give it a go, but I'm not entirely sure we're cut out for the job. Larry, I think you have to stay here. I can't believe I'm saying this, but – gulp – *I'LL GO.'*

Toto hugged her brother and touched noses. Yes, he was cheeky, yes, he pretended to be a ninja and that did annoy her a bit, plus he always he licked butter straight off the plate under the noses of Mamma and Papa when they weren't looking, BUT he was a great big brother, the bravest there was.

'OK, bro, take a deep breath and hang on to me. If we get separated, head straight for the surface and don't panic.'

Toto could tell her brother was nervous, but there was no backing out now. *TOTO AND SILVER EACH TOOK A LUNGFUL OF COOL EVENING AIR, AND DIVED IN.*

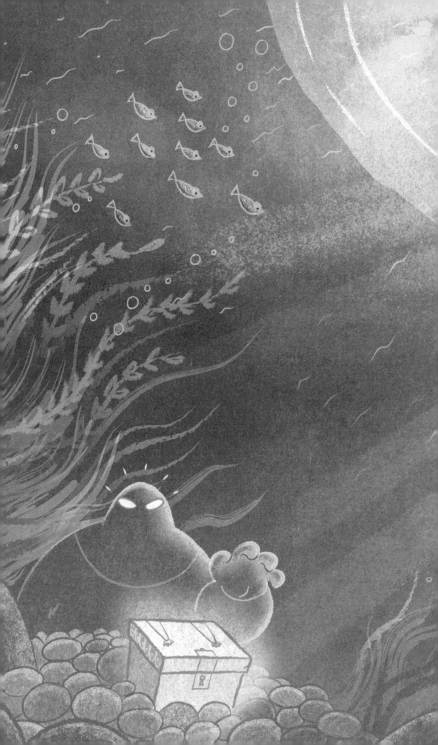

The little ninja kicked powerfully, and it was clear that the training she'd had from her otter friend had paid off. She ploughed down through the water and, before long, they reached the pond bed. Silver was hanging on for dear life, but he was surprised how quickly he adjusted to the cold and the weightlessness of being underwater.

Silver started to look around to spot where the collar could be, but each time he moved his feet he stirred up rotten leaves and mud that made the water murky and clouded his view. He was beginning to get desperate, and short of breath. Just as he was about to make Toto kick for the surface, a chink of light from the moon above reflected off the bottom of the pond. **SOMETHING WAS THERE!**

Directing his sister, they swam over to the source of the reflection and there it was: faded and rusty, but it was unmistakeably the corner of a **SILVER BOX,** buried in the mud and untouched for hundreds of years. Silver grabbed it triumphantly and Toto started to swim them upwards.

Suddenly, she felt something snag below her. Looking down, she couldn't make out much, but she could tell **SOMEONE HAD A HOLD ON SILVER** and was trying to wrestle the box away from him, pulling them all down towards the bottom. Toto tried to drag her brother towards the surface, but she was almost out of breath and her strength was depleted. She tugged once more at her brother, who looked up at her as she gestured upwards. Frustrated but feeling dizzy and out of breath, Silver could tell she was right: it was either them or the box. Reluctantly he let go of the prize and watched as a **SHADY FIGURE IN A WETSUIT MADE FROM RUBBER GLOVES** and wearing goggles kicked powerfully and disappeared into the dark water.

The two cats surfaced and gasped for air. Toto could just about make out the dark shapes of her friends on the bank. She cradled her brother and swam over to where the others were waiting.

Collapsing on the grass, Silver looked up to his sister. 'I'm sorry, whatever that was down there was so strong. I thought I'd be able to fight it off, but it had such a hold on me. I felt like I was going to black out.'

'Don't worry, it looks like we got you out just in time,' Toto answered.

'What now, though?' said Catface. 'Whoever it was is obviously the same cad who attacked me in Larry's office.'

'Look, over there!' Socks interrupted. 'On the other side!'

THE CATS ALL TURNED TO SEE THE DARK FIGURE EMERGE FROM THE POND. It had its back to them so its face was obscured. It peeled off the wetsuit and they could see it was a **PURE WHITE RAT.** But something strange was happening: it looked like **IT WAS GAINING IN SIZE!** It was like nothing any of them had ever seen before. It grew to at least twice the size of Catface, and was sleek and powerful. The rodent stood upright on its back legs and went to disappear into the bushes, but then stopped, sensing something.

'It knows we're here,' whispered Larry.

Sure enough, the huge muscly rat turned and with an evil grin gave the cats a wave and pointed to its neck, where Old Tom's Collar was shining in the moonlight.

'*MONSIEUR RATON LAVEUR, THE FRENCH AMBASSADOR!' SILVER GASPED.*

'But he looks so different. *Mamma mia*, wearing that collar beefs him up a bit!'

'I simply refuse to believe it,' said Catface. 'He came to my show in Paris – charming man. **WE ATE A BAKED CAMEMBERT TOGETHER.** I told him to pay a visit over

here, see the sights. And as ambassador I thought he'd get a special tour of the Tower to see Old Tom's Collarrrrrr ...' He trailed off, aghast, and put his paw to his forehead. 'Hang on a minute ... I think I might have given him the idea ... Blast, sorry ...'

THE WHITE RAT LEERED TRIUMPHANTLY at the gang, and then turned and disappeared into the bushes.

Toto was the first to snap herself out of the stupor and took charge. 'Don't blame yourself, Catface; you weren't to know. The lengths that he's gone to prove he's an evil genius. **THE MOST IMPORTANT THING NOW IS TO WORK OUT WHERE HE'S HEADED.'**

'I think I can guess,' answered the glum

Catface. 'If he has united the two halves of Old Tom's Collar he'll want to mobilise an army. So he'll head for the nearest rat town: **HE'LL BE GOING TO RATBOROUGH!'**

CHAPTER 8

'So, let me get this straight,' puffed Silver as the team sprinted along the sewer that would get them to Ratborough. 'You reckon the nice, polite diplomat we've been guarding is actually a **CRIMINAL GENIUS** who, thanks to Catface (sorry, Catface), has been plotting all along to swipe Old Tom's Collar, and raise an army of every rat in the country to do his bidding.'

'Well, as crazy as it sounds, yes!' answered
Toto.

'Honestly, sis, *HE'S AS BIG AS A SIBERIAN
CAT,* not an ounce of fat on him, very tough-
looking,' chipped in Socks.

'Not helpful, Socks! So, boss, what are
your orders when we get there?' she called
to Larry.

'The key will be to isolate him. It's vital we
get him away from the townsfolk as quickly
as possible, so he can't turn them. Then you
and I will take him on. I thought it was just
legend, but he really did seem to grow in
size and stature when he put on both pieces
of the collar. He could be lethal in combat;
we'll have to approach with caution.'

Up ahead, Catface was leading the way to Ratborough – the rat capital of north London, and the seat of his father's power. To avoid the crowds, Catface took the back route but a couple of times they heard a squadron of rat soldiers marching towards them, and hid in the shadows, uncertain as to whose side they were on. Finally, they made it to the town square, and lurked in a side street that the cats knew well. Peeking out from behind a wall made of old soup tins, they took in the scene.

'Oh, this is not good. As in, it's bad,' said Silver with a wince, as he painted the picture for Toto.

All the townsfolk were in the square and their eyes were on the grand old palace made from glass bottles that dominated the skyline. **UP ON THE BALCONY WAS CATFACE'S DAD, THE KING RAT.** But he wasn't addressing his people. He was surrounded by his own guards, who were armed with toothpicks. It was clear he was under arrest. Monsieur Raton Laveur (if that was his real name) was proudly addressing the crowd. His voice now had no shred of a French accent. He was finally showing his true colours, and the rats were hanging on every word.

'My friends, for years you have been lied to by cowards and traitors.' He gestured to the king.

'I say, steady on,' said the king.

'SILENCE!' the giant rat continued, 'All the animals in the kingdom look down upon

us rats, they laugh and sneer at us, think us dirty and diseased. Well, no more!'

THE CROWD ERUPTED IN APPRECIATION.

'When my great-great-great-great-great-great ...' (this was repeated for another thirty seconds and even the most committed listeners were beginning to look a little distracted) '...
GREAT-GRANDFATHER, KING RODERICK THE ABSOLUTELY FILTHY DIRTY, was betrayed by his own kind and defeated by Old Tom, my family went into hiding in Europe, but we've never forgotten our destiny. We have been biding our time, waiting for centuries to come again and claim what is rightfully ours.'

A shout of support went up from the square. Behind the old soup tins, the cats heard every word.

'And now is that time. From this day forth, **I WILL BE KNOWN AS KING RODERICK THE SPOTLESSLY CLEAN.** I hold the sacred collar of Old Tom; I am your rightful sovereign and I command you to follow me and do my bidding. Together we will unite all the rats and pigeons in the country and take our revenge on the rest of animal kind!'

'He's off his rocker ... We have to act fast, and get that collar off him. Any ideas as to how we can get him separated from this mob?' Toto asked. 'We don't stand a chance if we're up against the whole town. We'll be destroyed.'

'I say, that guard over there.' Catface gestured to a small rat on the fringes of the crowd. 'I do believe that's Terry. Yes, I went to school with him. Not the brightest, but a lovely fellow. I'm sure I can get him to help.' He stood up from their hiding place and called, 'Terry, yoo-hoo.'

'**CATFACE, NO!**' Toto hissed, but it was too late. Terry turned to see Catface waving, although now with a little less certainty. The guard narrowed his eyes, but started to walk over to where the group were hiding.

'See?' Catface beamed to his friend. 'Good old Terry, never lets you down.'

'THEY'RE HERE! TRAITORS, OVER HERE!' the rat shouted as loud as he could.

'Oh blast ... well, I did say he wasn't the sharpest at school,' Catface lamented.

The townsfolk turned and stared in the direction of Catface and the gang. Up above them, a malevolent grin spread across Roderick's face. 'Rats of Ratborough, my first command to you is to hunt these traitors down. NONE SHALL LIVE!'

Slowly, as if they were one creature, the whole town started walking towards the gang, chanting over and over again, 'None shall live, none shall live.'

'CATFACE, GET US OUT OF HERE. NOW!' Larry said hurriedly.

'Yes, I do think that might be a wise course of action. This way, friends!'

The cat-rat disappeared through a crack in the wall next to the square. The cats followed him and found themselves in a warren of small tight alleyways, with first floor dwellings that jutted out overhead.

The dark alleys were the perfect place to stay out of sight as they rushed to escape above ground – though they could hear the rumbling footsteps of the rat army, never far away.

Finally, they emerged from the alleyways at a steep rock face where a narrow path ascended sharply. It seemed like they'd lost the mob, but they knew they couldn't rest, they had to be careful as one stumble could send them tumbling down the cliff into the abyss below. They formed a line and held on to each other's tails,

as Catface navigated the slippery rock.

After a while, Ratborough became visible far beneath them, the torches of the town shining in the darkness. The winding path they were following then seemed to even out and with one more turn they saw an old viaduct dead ahead, with a wide underground white-water river foaming underneath

its arches.

'It's from the Victorian era, built around the same time as the animal Tube.

It got condemned years ago as it's falling apart, but it's the only way to get out from here, so we have to go across carefully, one or two at a time,' Catface advised.

'Once we're out, **WE HAVE TO GET SHEILA AND HER POLICE DOGS DOWN HERE ASAP AND SHE'LL SEE THE TRUTH!** Then we can deal with King Roderick, or Monsieur Raton Laveur or whoever this cad is,' ordered Larry. 'Toto, you and Silver OK to take point? And I'll guard the back.'

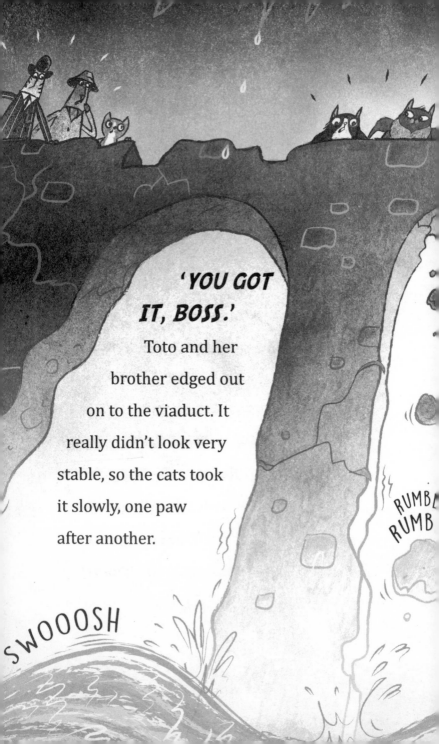

'YOU GOT IT, BOSS.'

Toto and her brother edged out on to the viaduct. It really didn't look very stable, so the cats took it slowly, one paw after another.

RUMBLE
RUMB

SWOOOSH

They had crossed halfway and were feeling pretty confident. 'Not far to go now, sis,' said Silver, looking ahead. Even with her ninja skills on high alert,

WHOOOSH

she was grateful for her brother's support. **BUT ALL OF A SUDDEN, SILVER FROZE IN FEAR.** There was a huge figure looming out of the shadows on the far side of the bridge, dashing their hopes of a safe crossing.

'Oh no.' Silver sighed, defeated. 'It's him.'

KING RODERICK WALKED SLOWLY AND WITH STEELY PURPOSE TOWARDS THE PAIR. The old viaduct began to moan and rumble; it was clear it wouldn't hold all their weight for long. The huge white rat stopped a short distance away, looked down on the two small cats and sneered. 'So, here she is, Old Tom's heir-in-waiting, and her "seeing eye" cat. Pathetic. I have to say, I expected better. Old Tom was our mortal enemy, but he was a worthy opponent, not the runt of the litter.'

SILVER HISSED AT THE TOWERING RODENT and made to attack him, but Toto held her brother back. Even now, with all the odds stacked against him, he still had her back, and she couldn't love him more. 'No, bro.' She shook her head.

'*No, bro,*' the rat mimicked Toto. 'Wise advice, but it won't do you any good. I'm going to tear her limb from limb, then you, then Larry. All of you! Tom's disciples, you stupid pathetic ninjas will be destroyed and I'll be free to complete my destiny!' He laughed.

'He really has got some anger issues,' Silver whispered to his sister. 'So, sis, any ideas how you're going to play this one?' He tried to sound as breezy as he could, but

Toto could tell he was scared, and with good reason. So was she. She couldn't remember when she'd faced an adversary as physically intimidating. Roderick was huge, but it wasn't only that – there was something about the way he carried himself that just made him seem invincible.

He stomped towards them and with every step the bridge shook. It started to feel like it was about to crumble – it was clear the old viaduct simply couldn't take the weight.

RUMBLE
RUMBLE

As the cats backed away from Roderick, Toto could feel the ground starting to give way from underneath them. **THE PART OF THE VIADUCT WHERE THEY STOOD WAS COLLAPSING!** Sensing she had to act fast, Toto picked her brother up and hurled him back over to the safety of the cliff where the rest of the gang, who were safe and sheltered, caught him.

'*Grazie!*' Silver called.

TOTO THEN JUST HAD ENOUGH TIME TO DIVE THE OTHER WAY – TOWARDS RODERICK! – before the part of the viaduct she had been standing on disappeared into the river below, in a shower of dusty debris.

Toto stood up and dusted herself down. **HER BROTHER WAS SAFE, BUT SHE WAS ANYTHING BUT.**

CHAPTER 9

'Finally, I get to avenge my great-great-great-great great-great ...' (once again this was repeated for thirty seconds, to the point where everyone was getting a little embarrassed) '... great-grandfather, and wipe Tom's heir from the face of the earth. Then nothing will stop me from mobilising every rat and pigeon in the country to rise up and take back what is rightfully theirs!'

'*Coo, coo*, excuse me, do you think we could we chip in?'

The tension was momentarily dampened as everyone looked around to where two pigeons were nesting in the rock face above the viaduct.

'COO-EE, YES, UP HERE, SORRY TO

BOTHER YOU – the name's Cora. This is my husband, Michael.' Michael simply nodded his head in a pigeon-like way. 'Now, we just couldn't help overhearing you mentioned pigeons, and as **MEMBERS OF THE PIGEON EQUALITY PARTY,** we thought we should let you know that **WE ALL REJECTED THE LEGEND OF OLD TOM'S COLLAR YEARS AGO.** We're quite happy as we are, thank you very much, all getting on nicely. So, if you'd be so kind, **PLEASE LEAVE ALL THE PIGEONS OUT OF IT.** Now, I'll let you get back to whatever you were doing. Come on now, Michael, I've got a seed risotto on the hob ... ta ra, everyone.' Cora disappeared back into the nest and, after nodding a couple of times, Michael followed suit.

All the animals below didn't quite know what to do or where to look!

Toto piped up first. 'Err, right, OK, so back to it. Let's say the plan worked, what then?' she asked, knowing that if he opened up, she might find a way to get to Roderick.

'I have to be honest, I haven't really given the next stage of the plan an awful lot of thought.' He sighed, still distracted by the pigeons' interruption, and momentarily letting his guard down. 'I don't know. Get a nice castle, start a family ... But never mind that!' he yelled, shaking his head. 'All that matters is this!' He pointed to the collar he was proudly wearing. '*ALL THESE STUPID RATS WILL FOLLOW ME AND DO WHAT I TELL THEM TO DO SO LONG AS I HAVE*

OLD TOM'S COLLAR IN MY POSSESSION.'

'Yes, I've been meaning to ask you about that.' Toto desperately tried to think of something else to ask the mighty rat. 'We, err, umm, all understand the promise of revenge your ancestor made, but why has it taken six hundred years for your family to come back?'

'It's all down to that idiot,' he said, pointing to Catface.

'Oh dear, I had a feeling this might be the case. *Meow culpa*.' Catface grimaced.

'For years I have been plotting how to get close to Old Tom's Collar, but like my forefathers, I found every option was hopeless. **THE SAPPHIRES AND THE RIDDLE WERE SO WELL GUARDED,** they were impossible to get to. So, I've been masquerading as the French Ambassador for the last year, biding my time, seeing where and when I could make my move. And all the while seeing relations between cats and rats improve every day, thanks to you, Toto, Catface, and your merry band of friends. I knew I had to act soon, or it would be too late. Everyone is getting on so well, it's sickening! Then I went to see Catface play in Paris, and over a baked Camembert he told me that, as ambassador, I should request to see the collar when I visited. A request from a diplomat couldn't be turned down ...'

'Sorrrrryyyy again,' groaned Catface.

'And that's when my plan was hatched. From there it was easy: I sent Cyril drugged blood biscuits anonymously. The fool couldn't resist them. I waited for him to pass out, then I broke into his bedroom, stole the key, retrieved MY collar, put the key back, and waited for the perfect crime to be pinned on Cyril and Larry. That buffoon Fluffypaws has been looking for an excuse to get rid of the ninjas and the ravens, when they are the only thing keeping animals and humans alike safe and sound. His idiocy has served my purpose. With Larry out of the way I could break into his safe, and *voila*! The perfect crime was committed!'

Larry was seething with rage, but it was Catface who spoke next.

'**HANG ON, YOU MEAN TO SAY YOU'RE NOT ACTUALLY THE FRENCH**

AMBASSADOR?' Catface looked aghast.

'Of course not – I kidnapped him ages ago, sent him to Corsica (to be fair he's having a great life, chargrilled tuna every day), and since then I've taken over his identity and fooled everyone into believing I am the charming Monsieur Raton Laveur.' He made a grandiose bow. 'When in actual fact *I AM KING RODERICK THE SPOTLESSLY CLEAN.'*

'Why not "the Filthy Dirty" like your ancestor?' Toto asked.

'Argh!!!! NO! I hate dirt, all of it. The filthy mud, sewage and soil that my poor ancestors had to root around in to eke out an existence because of the likes of you. Well, no more! From this day forth rats will be known as spotlessly clean.'

'Well, he's got one thing right there – we are a clean bunch, terribly misunderstood. He's obviously mad, but you can't fault his logic,' said Catface.

'Enough, you blithering fool! Come, Toto, it's time for you to fulfil my destiny.'

Before Toto could make a move, a flash of tabby fur flew past her in the direction of Roderick.

'I'LL TEACH YOU TO RUIN MY NAME!' It was Larry. He'd taken a running jump and landed on the viaduct. Aiming a kick at Roderick, he connected with the giant rat's chest. Normally, this **DEADLY NINJA KICK** would have sent an opponent flying, but Larry **SIMPLY BOUNCED OFF RODERICK.** Smiling with

malevolence, the rat picked up a stunned Larry and threw him backwards, knocking him clean out.

Larry is the greatest ninja of all time! If he can't defeat Roderick, what chance have I got? Toto thought to herself.

'Shall we?' the rat sneered at Toto.

She could make out Larry lying in a crumpled heap and she had no idea what to do. Her only option was to **RELY ON HER NINJA INSTINCTS AND STAY CALM.** She launched herself through the air and aimed a kick at Roderick, which he ducked. She aimed again, but he deflected her hardest blow. She tried to get in close and do some damage that way, but he seemed to soak up everything she threw at him: a punch here,

179

a kick there, nothing worked. In exchange, he was **DELIVERING PAINFUL BLOWS** to the little ninja.

Owww! This guy is so tough and fast, if I don't find a weakness soon I'm done for, Toto thought to herself, as the rat picked her up and hurled her across the viaduct too. As she landed, she kicked a cloud of dust into the air from the crumbling brickwork.

Roderick looked appalled as some of it landed on his fur.

BOSH

'Urgh, disgusting.'
He quickly patted
himself down and
closed in on Toto.

She was bruised,
tired and sore, but
this was the one
chink in his armour
she'd been looking for.
Of course! He hates dirt! So, as the ninja
got up for her last stand, she grabbed a
handful of dirt.

'Playtime is
over – time for
you to go for
a dip,' the rat
snarled at her.

'Actually, I think you're the one who might need a wash,' she replied as she let fly with her handful of dirt and hit him square on the chest.

'ARGH! YOU DIRTY LITTLE CAT, I'M FILTHY! Come here – you're a dead kitty now.'

Toto knew that if she could get him so annoyed with the mud-slinging then she might, just might, stand a chance.

He lunged for her, and she dived out of the way, throwing another handful of dirt as she dodged his blow. Again and again she dived out of the way of his punches with a millisecond to spare, and each time she was able to connect with another handful of dusty earth that enraged the giant rat.

The others were helping, getting in on the action from afar. They hurled mud from the edge of the viaduct and, eventually, the white rat was so covered in dust, muck and mud that he looked more brown than white. He was tired and furious, but still deadly. One last time, *TOTO WENT TO HURL A PAWFUL OF MUD AT THE RAT,* but this time he was too quick; he grabbed her by her foot, and spun her around like he was throwing a hammer on an athletics field. *CRASHING INTO THE ANCIENT VIADUCT,* next to a still knocked-out Larry, she could feel the structure vibrate under her. It wasn't going to last much longer, but her foot was really sore and she wasn't sure if she could stand.

Toto looked up to see the enormous rat

standing over her. **'LOOKS LIKE YOUR LUCK HAS RUN OUT, NINJA.'** He raised his arm, but both the rat and the ninja were momentarily distracted by a break in the shadowy light.

A call came from the darkness. 'I think you'll find you're the one who's run out of luck!' Before Roderick could even see where the owner of the voice was, a **FLASH OF BLACK FEATHERS** flitted across Toto's eyeline and **SHARP TALONS TORE OLD TOM'S COLLAR FROM RODERICK'S NECK.**

'CYRIL! YOU LEGEND!' shouted Silver from the cliff. Toto was on her feet in a second – her leg was in agony, but without Old Tom's Collar she could tell Roderick was now very vulnerable.

'*NOOOOOOOO, YOU MEDDLING RAVEN!* You were locked up! How did you escape? I'll pluck your feathers right now!'

But Cyril was safely perched on the cliff face, and, crucially, so was the collar.

In the days to come, those who witnessed it said that *WITHOUT THE COLLAR RODERICK LOOKED LIKE HE VISIBLY SHRANK.* Toto had no idea if this was true – all she knew was that without it, he finally seemed beatable.

With her last ounce of strength, she launched a kick that sent him flying towards the edge of the crumbling viaduct. Getting to his feet, he made one last effort to spring at Toto, but the bricks began to fall from under his feet. Toto saw what was happening and dived to help him, but it was too late. **THE RAT TUMBLED DOWN INTO THE RAGING RIVER BELOW,** and disappeared under the surface.

Toto had no time to feel bad; she had to save herself and Larry. **THE REST OF THE VIADUCT WAS COLLAPSING** and there was no way she could lift Larry and jump to safety.

'Your number's not up yet, little lady – hold on!' Toto turned to find Cyril swooping in from the shadows. **'GRAB LARRY, AND JUMP '** the old raven cried.

Toto launched into the darkness as the old viaduct gave way, and for a second they were freefalling, plunging towards the torrent of water below.

JUST AS SHE THOUGHT IT WAS TOO LATE, SHE FELT THE IRON GRIP OF CYRIL'S MIGHTY TALONS AROUND HER SHOULDERS AND SHE AND LARRY WERE BEING CARRIED TO THE SAFETY OF THE CLIFF EDGE TO BE REUNITED WITH THEIR FRIENDS.

CHAPTER 10

Getting out of Ratborough had been a doddle. Pretty much as soon as the collar had been ripped from Roderick, **SHEILA HAD TURNED UP WITH THE CIA** and the mob had dispersed, looking a bit embarrassed and apologetic. As the cats made their way back down the path, there were a good few remarks of 'Sorry about that' and 'Not sure what came over us'.

Catface's dad, however, was having none of it. 'My office NOW!' he screamed at his aides. It was pretty clear there would be hell to pay for the mutiny.

'Oh, those poor rats, they'll be cleaning his throne room for a month!' Catface winced.

THE CATS LAUGHED, SHOOK THEIR HEADS AND GOT OUT OF RATBOROUGH AS QUICKLY AS POSSIBLE.

Now they had possession of Old Tom's Collar, Cyril and Larry wanted to get it **BACK UNDER LOCK AND KEY** right away. Even with Roderick seemingly out of the picture, the gang still couldn't relax until they **GOT IT TO THE TOWER.** Once they were safely back in the turret room, Cyril placed it in the cabinet.

OLD TOM'S
COLLAR

As he was doing so, Silver turned to his sister. 'Be honest, would you like to have worn it just once so we could speak to humans? Imagine the fun we could have winding up Mamma and Papa!'

'Bro, we have enough trouble trying to make sense of animals – don't even get me started on humans,' she said, giving him a nudge.

Cyril carefully and deliberately placed one key, attached to a necklace, around his neck, and handed the other to Larry with a solemn nod. The cat did the same. They gang gazed up at the two bands of Old Tom's Collar – reunited, but firmly locked away behind bullet-, paw- and claw-proof glass. **'I 'VE TRIPLED THE GUARD DUTY** and this key will never leave my side. Plus, that new enforced glass should do the trick,' the raven declared.

'Are you sure we shouldn't hide it away, bury it somewhere? The power it holds over my species is frightening,' Catface said, in a moment of contemplation.

'If we do that, then the likes of Roderick will have won,' Cyril answered with a sad smile. 'The animal world has never been safer and more harmonious than now. This is a symbol of that harmony, and I want to fight to keep it that way. With the help of everyone in this room, we will. Now then' – he clapped his wings together – **'TIME FOR A CELEBRATION. BLOOD BISCUITS FOR ALL!'**

Cyril clicked his talons and a set of doors opened that led to a Tudor dining room with a table full of roast beef and all the trimmings, cheesy pasta (for Toto) and bowls and bowls of blood biscuits.

'Though I might give them a miss, just for today,' Cyril whispered to Toto.

As the gang tucked in, Cyril updated them on how he had got out of the Tower. 'When Larry escaped, I squawked and squawked

until Sheila came to the room. Well, you know I said I felt groggy – I suddenly remembered the anonymous biscuits and I asked her to check them. Sure enough, they'd been drugged to send me to sleep.'

'Plus,' added Sheila, sheepishly, 'my team told me your office had been ransacked when they arrived, Larry, so we knew something wasn't right with Fluffypaws' theory. That was enough for me. Sorry I had to go so heavy earlier; I was under orders.'

'Oh, don't worry about that.' Larry smiled. 'You were just doing your job – I'd have done the same. Well, maybe I wouldn't have locked me up, but you know ...'

'**WHERE IS OLD FLUFFYPAWS, BY THE WAY?** Doesn't seem like him to miss out on the glory,' said Socks.

'Oh, he ran back to the House of Commons as soon as he heard about your innocence. Apparently, the prime minister is furious with him. I don't think we'll be seeing him for a while.'

'**WELL, *I* FOR ONE WILL DRINK TO THAT,**' said Silver as he chinked a goblet of milk with Socks.

The gang all tucked into the feast and there was a sense of relief in the room as old friendships seemed to be mended and solidified. Toto helped herself to a bowl of cheesy pasta and sat down next to Larry.

'I want to thank you, Toto; you've taught me a lesson.'

'What? Larry, you're my boss and my sensei – you don't have to thank me. You're the one teaching me, not the other way around!'

'No – on the viaduct, I let my pride get the better of me once again, and that was my undoing. I was so enraged at Roderick for framing me, I let it cloud my judgement, and he took advantage of that. If you hadn't been there, I don't think there'd have been anyone else to stop him ... I owe you a debt.'

'Don't mention it, boss. Just glad to be of service.' She took a sip of milk. 'There is one thing I'm uneasy about, though.'

'*RODERICK?*' asked Larry, and Toto nodded. 'I'm the same. My instinct is telling me that's not the last we'll see of him. Even without Old Tom's Collar, he's a powerful adversary. But on the plus side, I for one can't wait to get even if he does show up again!' He smiled wickedly and knocked back a glass of milk. 'After all, how can he possibly hope to beat this motley *CREW OF HEROIC MISFITS: A WISE OLD RAVEN, TWO CHEEKY BUT COURAGEOUS BROTHERS, THE MOST LOYAL POLICE DOG, THE MOST KNOWLEDGEABLE AND CHARMING CAT-RAT EVER TO WALK THE STREETS OF LONDON, AND*

THE BEST NINJA I HAVE EVER SEEN.
Who could possibly compete with that?'

He gave Toto a reassuring hug, then turned back to the party. Toto looked out of the turret window, where she could just about make out pinpricks of light from the stars in the night sky. If Roderick was out there, she'd be ready, along with all her friends. She stayed still for a couple of minutes more, then re-joined those she loved the most.

EPILOGUE

The muddy, silty sewer spewed into the Thames through a storm drain, right on the outskirts of London where the river began to flow into the sea. Its contents included half a brick viaduct and one **RODERICK** the Spotlessly Clean, who, right now, was anything but clean! It was safe to say, he wasn't best pleased.

'**_I AM FILTHY DIRTY, JUST LIKE MY POOR FOREFATHERS,_**' he moaned out loud as he swam to the bank of the river.

'Argh! I had it all, all in my grasp. My destiny! And that runt of the litter and an old raven stole it from me. *OH, THEY'LL PAY FOR THIS ...* I'll be feasting on raven pie for a week! And as for Toto, she'll be glad she's blind when she sees what I've got in store for her.'

He shook the water from his fur and tried his hardest to dry out. Toto and Larry were right: even without the collar he was strong. The only things wounded were his *PRIDE AND HIS SPOTLESS COAT.*

Roderick was still wringing himself dry when he heard a rustle from the nearby bushes. He immediately got himself into *FIGHTING MODE,* thinking that Toto had followed him. But as he looked closer, he realised it was a cat he'd never seen before, dressed in a *STUNNING BLACK*

VELVET CAPE AND A TOP HAT. He was leaning up against the wall, silently taking Roderick in, while cleaning his paws.

'STAY BACK, CAT. I WARN YOU, I'M NOT IN THE MOOD.'

The cat didn't seem to pay any heed to the warning and emerged from the shadows, skulking towards him.

'That's no way to greet a friend. **RELAX!** I mean you no harm. Quite the contrary – I believe we might have some **ARCH-ENEMIES** in common. Now, first things first, let's get you warm and dry ... I say, care for some fondue?' the stranger said, ushering the rat to a disused river houseboat nearby.

'But ... who are you?' the rat asked.

'OH, ME? THE NAME'S FERDICAT, AS IN ARCHDUKE. AND TOGETHER, MY NEW CHUM, I THINK WE MIGHT DO SOME TERRIBLE THINGS TOGETHER.

MMEEEOOOWWWW

THE END

DID YOU KNOW THAT THERE ARE THREE OTHER TOTO ADVENTURES?

TOTO
THE NINJA CAT
AND THE GREAT SNAKE ESCAPE

DERMOT O'LEARY
ILLUSTRATED BY NICK EAST

TOTO
THE NINJA CAT
AND THE INCREDIBLE CHEESE HEIST

DERMOT O'LEARY

ILLUSTRATED BY NICK EAST

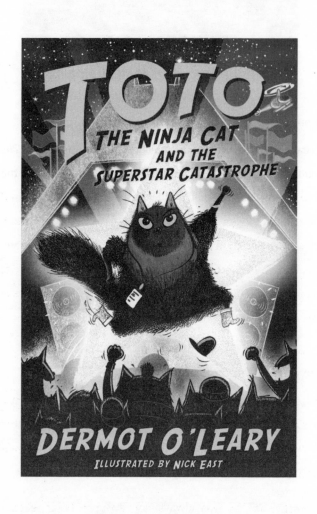

AND THEY'RE ALSO AVAILABLE AS AUDIO BOOKS,
READ BY DERMOT HIMSELF!

AUTHOR Q AND A
MEET DERMOT!

What made you want to write children's books?

I really enjoyed writing a book for grown-ups called *The Soundtrack to My Life* a couple of years before I started the *Toto* series. Then my wife and I got a couple of cats, Toto and Silver, and I thought this would make a lovely idea for a book for younger readers. I get on really well with my niece – she was 9 when I started on *Toto* – and I know what her sense of humour is like. So I figured I'd write with her in mind – she was my audience.

Did you enjoy reading as a child?

Yes, and both my parents are big readers. My dad is great – he's a born storyteller. He read us old Irish fairy stories that he was passing on. He even wrote a little book about two owls for my niece when she was younger.

Fantastic Mr Fox was always my favourite book when I was growing up. I also really loved Raymond Briggs – *The Snowman* and *Father Christmas* especially.

Did you have pets when you were growing up?

No cats, but we had a rabbit growing up, and I was devastated when it died. The greatest moment of treachery in my whole life was when my Mum and Dad moved house from the village I grew up in and they said I could have a dog. Then as soon as they moved they reneged on it. Oh it was awful!

Like the hero of your book, your real pet cat Toto is blind isn't she?

We worked out quite quickly that our Toto couldn't really see that well. We took her to the vet and found she had no red blood cells in her eyes. They told us the camera is there, but there's no film in it, so she can see breaks in light but not much else.

We noticed really quickly though that Toto had lightning fast reactions; if you were playing around she could just lash out with her claws, super swift. I thought this would make a great idea for a book: that one cat is a lovely, mild-mannered kitten during the day – and then a Ninja by night!

ACKNOWLEDGEMENTS

As always, we have to start with the stars of the show: Toto, Silver and Socks.

Cats are good, they should run the world ... maybe ADF was right all long ... curses.

To my partner in ink, Nick East. I am doubly blessed to have found such a gifted illustrator who is also an excellent human being. Thank you, and we will go walking in Yorkshire one day, promise. I'll bring the wine, and sausages.

To my uber-mensch team at Hachette Children's:

I honestly don't know where I'd be without them, actually I do ... unpublished.

Kate Agar (Katherine, if we are going regal ... which we should) you are a marvel. Wise, diplomatic, loyal, smart, brave and funny, with just the right amount of cavalier sprit. You would have made an excellent musketeer.

To Alison Padley, for her services to illustration and design and general cup half fullness. Her vision, creativity and positivity should be bottled and sold. She'd make a fortune.

To Anne McNeil, who fills me with nothing but warmth and support every time I see her, and always makes me feel valued as part of the team and the family.

To Fritha Lindquist, for your inexhaustible, passion, smarts, organisation, patience, and devotion to the children's book world and independent booksellers.

Also, an honourable mention in dispatches has to go to these folks and their teams:

From Editorial: Amina Youssef

Those cats in Marketing: Fiona Evans and Aashfaria Anwar

Big love to the brass section in Publicity: Lucy Clayton and Rebecca Logan

On drums (Production): Helen Hughes

You heard the word on Sales: Nicola Goode and Jennifer Hudson

Fighting for my rights: Eshara Wijetunga

And ... from the big bad world of Licensing: Karen Lawler and Sarah Lennon Galavan

If I've missed anyone out, I shall banish myself from Carmelite towers and never eat a morsel of your excellent cakes again.

To John, Jonny and Rob at my long-time agents John Noel Management. Thanks for cracking my Bletchley-code-like diary and finding time for me to write Toto, and for always having my back. And to Chloe for keeping the engine room going.

To Liz, Jordan, Imogen at LMPR, who handle my publicity with class, care and grace, always.

Massive thank-yous also to the following, who were hugely helpful in my research:

Chief Yeoman Warder at HM Tower of London (which if, like me, you love history, you must visit), Pete McGowran, who was so generous with his time, knowledge and expertise and unknowingly inspired the character of Cyril.

Emily Brazee, Meriel Jeater and Iona Ball at the Museum of London who helped me with my research into all things medieval London. This place is incredible, the most underrated of all of London's museums.

And thanks to the wonderful, poetic, joyous company of walking tour guide Simon Whitehouse. One of the London Blue Badge Tourist guides. We've been on two London walking tours with him now. I can't recommend it enough. It's the best way to see London and find out so much about our extraordinary city.

Thanks also to all the incredible book shops who have welcomed me with open arms ... and books. Especially the independent retailers, along with libraries – your value to your communities is immeasurable and for all to see.

And finally, thanks to Dee, for wise counsel, love and friendship. TKO always.

Dx

DERMOT O'LEARY'S

television and radio work has made
him a household name.

Dermot started his career on T4 for Channel 4
and has presented shows for both ITV and the BBC.
His best-known work includes ten series of The X Factor,
The National Television Awards, Big Brother's Little
Brother, Unicef's Soccer Aid, the RTS Award winning
'Live from Space' season and the Brit Awards which he
presented with Emma Willis in 2017.

In 2015 Dermot presented and co-produced Channel 4's
Battle of Britain, a two-part series commemorating
the 75th anniversary of one of the most pivotal
moments in British history.

2017 also saw Dermot launch his new Saturday morning
show on BBC Radio 2, 'Saturday Breakfast with
Dermot O'Leary'. Previously in the Saturday afternoon
slot, 'The Dermot O'Leary Show' won three Sony Radio
Awards and was well known for its support of new and
emerging bands. The show is produced by Ora Et Labora,
the production company Dermot co-founded in 2008.

Ora Et Labora also produces Rylan's BBC Radio 2 show,
a number of podcasts and the TV show 'Reel Stories', a
BBC2 show looking back at iconic singers' lives on
screen. Dermot has interviewed Kylie Minogue, Noel
Gallagher and Rod Stewart on the show so far, with more
episodes planned.

In 2018, Dermot joined Kirsty Young and Huw Edwards
to host the BBC's RTS Award winning coverage
of the Royal Wedding in front of an audience of
13 million people.

A huge Ernest Shackleton fan, in 2019 he presented
the 'Explorers' episode of the BBC's 'Icons: The Greatest
Person of the 20th Century'. His interview-based
podcast, 'People, Just People', launched with Audible
in 2019 and featured interviews with guests including
Stephen Graham, Ed Miliband and Eni Aluko.

Toto the Ninja Cat and the Mystery Jewel Thief is Dermot's
fourth children's book. He lives in London with his wife
Dee, their son Kasper, and their cats Socks and,
of course, Toto.